G

A novel by Joie Lamar

G

Cover design by Joie Lamar / Brainspired Publishing

No part of this book may be reproduced in any form or by any electronic or mechanical means including information storage and retrieval systems, without permission in writing from the author. The only exception is by a reviewer, who may quote short excerpts in review.

This book is a work of fiction. Names, character, places, and incidents are products of the author's imagination or are used fictitiously. Any resemblance to actual persons, living or dead, events, or locales, is entirely coincidental.

Visit my website at www.joielamar.com

Brainspired Publishing
A joint venture of Brainchild Holdings Inc. and INspired Media Inc.

Brainspired Publishing
Ontario, Canada
www.brainspiredpublishing.com

ISBN: 978-1-7774054-2-7

G

Also by Joie Lamar

Mambo Lips
Volume 1 - Memoir

Salsa Hips
Volume 2 - Memoir

Sapphoetry

Cuarenta y Nueve

(In collaboration with 48 additional artists)

Las Alas
(Co-Writer: a screenplay based on Joie Lamar's memoirs)

G
Currently in your hand
Volume 1– Detective Dan Cordova Crime Thriller Trilogy

See Whores
Volume 2 – Detective Dan Cordova Crime Thriller Trilogy
Q4 - 2022

DEDICATION

G, for Gangster, is dedicated to the 5 boroughs of New York; for you are each incredible teachers of culture, food, dance, language, style, attitude, and survival skills.

G

ACKNOWLEDGMENTS

Natalie. Always and forever my inspiration. Thank you for your undying support and love throughout all my creative endeavors. If there is ever an award for patience & understanding, it will be named after you, my love. Everything I do or create is because you shine your light and love on me.

To my 3,6,9 focus group; Sury Salem-Rosa, Kelly Hummell, Kate Johnston, Dallas Noftall, Dan Caudle, Antoine Elhashem, Lorenzo Pagnotta, Omar Ramirez, Sam Stratigeas, and Shayne Barbour-Ladak. I cannot tell you how important your opinions and suggestions were to the completion of this novel. Thank you for your brilliance and taking the time to help. You're all good people and cherished friends.

My fur babies who lie at my feet throughout every phase of every book I write, including when I trash an idea and swear, only to begin again. While your loyalty may be snack driven, I can't imagine writing anything without a wet nose mark on my notes and the unconditional love of my dogs.

Last, but not least, to my Mama. Writing about crime and evil in New York, albeit fiction, reminded me of all our safety talks during my childhood. Somehow you did not teach me to fear but to survive. You didn't encourage me to physically fight but to love, to be kind, and to rise above. I am more mentally strong than most, thanks to you. Today I can truly appreciate what a hell of a Mother you were. I miss you dearly, Rita. Thank you for encouraging me to write all my life. Somewhere, where your memories have gone to retire, I hope I make you proud.

G

PROLOGUE: When love slips through the cracks.

Children adapt wherever they are planted. Like abandoned roses growing through the concrete, they are beautifully resilient. It isn't until those fresh soft petals fall and the colors fade, that we notice the thorns left behind. If we are lucky the roots remain healthy, kept warm by a passion for survival, and those thorns become protective.

● ● ●

The light floated through the board slats that were meagerly nailed to what were once glass covered windows. This became my entertainment as a small child. I watched the rats follow this light striped pattern on the floor of my home for many hours before responding to my own hunger. They squeaked, stopped to watch us stretch and scrambled about frantically gathering breakfast. They were no longer shy about living amongst us and went about their daily life, as vermin, confidently. I was too young to know that we were much more vermin than the rats. It wasn't the squalor, or that we lived in an abandoned building, it was the absence of love that made us despicable. The adults, choked by addiction, consistently gasped for their next fix leaving us little ones to fend for ourselves. Oblivious to a life where parents feed their children, care for our needs, and or show us love; we went about our survival patterns every day without them. I don't remember feeling sad, or even deprived, just blank like a space needing to be filled.

We knew to walk around the adults gingerly, on our tip toes, while they traveled in and out of those drug induced stupors. I would often find food in my Mothers pockets while she lay intoxicated, with her eyes rolled back, drooling through the gaps of her missing teeth. Her stolen packages of Drakes Ho, Hos' fed my father's insatiable heroin related sweet tooth. Or as often was the case, she would sell them in exchange for some rock, her crack, but they were never ever meant to feed her hungry children directly. Something always fell out of their mouths when they ate, stoned, and I waited, a patient baby poised under any chin. Sometimes just sipping on the chocolate flavored dribble that fell my way.

As the children grew, they would often leave the confines of our abandoned building crack house and go hunting. The returned into the dark night with food and drink for us. Many began to exchange blow jobs for just enough money to pay for bags of potato chips and a six pack of Coke as early as the tender age of eight. It was never lost on me that a penis was the first kiss for many of the boys and girls that I grew up with. Entering your teenage years was often synchronized with entering juvenile detention, the foster care system, finding love from a pimp, selling your body, or inheriting your own addiction.

My Mother awoke from her crack fog long enough to show me love once. It wasn't in the form of affection, food, nurturing, or even words. She chose to give me up to the system, a back handed chance at a life outside of her crack and heroin world. I didn't cry when the police and social services took me away from her. The experience felt warm, soft, but still unnatural like the rats who nuzzled my neck at night to sleep.

And although what I have become since, and as an adult, lies on the periphery of her crack house, junkie life, I am grateful to my Mother for finding the strength to completely abandon me. I am a G, a Gangster, but I have risen above the way I was brought into the world and minimally raised.

My only addiction, ever, has been life.

G

G

FALLING TO MY DEATH

I've been in the Barclays Bank building in lower Manhattan many times but I am seeing it from a completely different perspective this time. The building façade glistens in the twilight. I can hear cars on the wet pavement. New York has a heartbeat even when all is still in the middle of the night.

Now I find myself floating to the ground, having been thrown from the rooftop of this high-rise building, to my death. What the fuck has happened? That's a rhetorical question since I will surely hit the ground before anyone can answer. I expect that I am propelling towards the street at a very high speed, but for me time is suspended. Interesting. I am somehow aware that it, time, mathematically speaking, no longer has meaning for me. It is true what they say, my life is flashing before my eyes as I descend. Slowly, like a movie that will end abruptly in a dark theatre, only there will be no fanfare to this ending. No credit roll. My life will end with a thump.

It is a street conversation that we gangsters have often, proudly, too afraid and immersed to understand it for what it is; an abbreviated life. I was born into this world of crime and short lives. I am a G, in every real sense; a Latina lesbian gangster. The last photo of me will be of my face smashed by the concrete. I should have taken more selfies to be remembered by.

The Gay mafia exist in all its hidden splendor in New York and various cities around the world. In the big apple, we have cored out the fashion industry, clubs, drugs, and yes, even Wall Street. Gangster life, but not in just the movie magic hetero way; We are hard core, dyke like, lipstick lesbians, and the many variations in between. We travel in all circles and as part of the sometimes unknowing, Pride flag waving, LGBT community. We control the street thugs hired into the industries that the gay mafia runs and owns. We are like unicorn sleeper cells bound to enforce rainbow law. Don't let the pretty colours fool you. It gets ugly on these mean streets.

My name is Sonny. I didn't realize what a rough year I was truly having until right at this 'plummeting to my death' moment. I should have paid full attention to the inspirational, stay positive, and be grateful posts on Facebook. It would not have changed my current situation, but I might have appreciated life more before this. I might have paid attention to my surroundings and possibly seen this coming.

The truth is that you don't have time to synchronize your cadence to normal everyday life in this world of crime. I work for Leticia Maldonado. She determines my schedule. I am one of the few G's who Leticia has allowed to deliver her deposits to wall street. She is going to miss me for sure but not as much as she will miss her deposit.

Great, I'm pissing on myself as I fall. My thoughts and body are completely disconnected. One knows it is going to die, and has completely given in to the fear of the thump. while the other contemplates the life that I will leave behind. I apologize for my thoughts becoming more and more random as of this point but I am, after all, falling to my death.

Everything I do, I do for Raya. How quickly she stole my heart. My soulmate. I know it sounds cliché but she came along and wet me from head to toe. It's true, my life was totally dehydrated before I met her. Please don't judge me for thinking about her as I urinate on myself.

She was "Pura" when we met. That means pure, in English, and what we call people outside of this criminal element. I loved that Raya had no idea of what went on in the background, in Greenwich village and the many "Gay-centric" areas of New York. She was my first normal sit down to dinner date kind of woman. It felt so easy and I felt so decent courting her. And besides wanting her body on that first date, I wanted this kind of life with her forever. It would take time for me to save up for the big disconnect, but scarier than all of that, I would have to let her in to my world; into my secrets. "Relationships are honest", Raya would often say. I loved her subtle invitation to be real, and open my heart, as much as I feared telling her everything.

Her face belied her shock the first time I told her about myself. That dirty, ugly, side of me. The person that often-left people bloodied and scared. And the Sonny who would have to kill you if Leticia so ordered it. The entire city is a front for money laundering, drugs, sex, and gun sales. It all passes through the almighty Leticia before the Italianos receive their nasty proceeds, minus her cut. That cut that pays me a living.

That Raya and I had just made love for 4 hours straight, and that she had screamed for God repeatedly, was probably the worst time to talk about murder, crime, and that I am a gangster. "What? You're not a courier?" she asked. A question equivalent to her having said "you lied to me". There is no sugar coating it and truly, no comforting way to tell it, now that I remember that day. Still, she accepted my lifestyle like a boss and we began to plan my departure from this life of indecency on the same day that we both professed our love for one another. It was a short one year plan and I was 6 months into it, almost to the minute, before finding myself on this trip South to Streetville.

My mind is drifting and an overwhelming feeling of sadness has replaced my fear of dying. I am sad for her. My sweet girl who often complained of the long boring nights at home without me, despite our plans. Raya will come home to find I haven't let Bullet, our Dachshund, out to poop. She will clean up his messes around the house, cursing my name, as she always does. She will rehearse her speech. The speech where she asks me to get rid of him as soon as I walk through the door. He will weave in and out of her legs in the excitement of welcoming her home while she pours herself a glass of wine. Bullet is our baby and neither one of us would let him go but when Raya gets angry at me she speaks such nonsense. Just a couple of sips of her wine and they will go about their normal evening routine while waiting for me to arrive home.

Let me stop for a dropping to my death PSA here: Political correctness dies while you're falling to your death, which is why I am not embarrassed to tell you that I feel the warmth of diarrhea making its way out of my ass. Is this how it ends? How long will my brain continue to review my life, after I've shit on someone looking up to see me nosedive in horror? But I digress…

We don't do normal dinner time in my house. Ironically, Raya has adjusted to this, while I plan that dream life of consistency. She does not ask questions but she knows that my hours are spent enforcing Leticia's law and running her nefarious errands. Dinner will be cooked without any expectation of what time we eat or where in the house we plant ourselves to do so. She will keep it warm for me. Bullet and that glass of wine will keep her company on the couch and chances are Raya will turn on the television to the news channel.

Perhaps she will recognize my Fila Ferrari shoes from under the coroners blanket over my body in the street. She always hated that I could spend $300 on sneakers and rightly so. Now they will end up in a box, on a dusty shelf, as evidence for a murder that will never be investigated. Gangsters die on the street like used condoms spill life into to our sewage systems in New York City. Our depravity for life comes back to haunt us in death, as it should.

My blood, shit, and piss will simply show up as wetness on the Wall Street cobblestone in tomorrow's newspaper. No one will bat an eye once the body is removed. The stench will not be any more or any less. She won't really put it together until the police or Leticia call her. This will warrant that ugly cry of hers. The kind of crying that I tease her about when we watch The Notebook together.

I wish that I could tell her how sorry I was that I did not keep my daily morning promise to be careful. That even from the depths of hell, where I am surely going, I will regret not getting to marry my beautiful Raya. That all that Salsa practice we spent hours and money on would not give birth to our first dance on our wedding day with the whole family watching in awe, as we so often dreamed of together.

I can't control how I will hit the ground. I pray that something, anything that I have done right in this lifetime will at least determine my body placement on these cold wet streets of the city that never sleeps. I don't want to land on a car and trigger an alarm that wakes everyone up. Just a quiet dignified fall would be nice.

Regardless, Leticia will see my picture in the morning paper and she will refer to me as another broken puppet on her streets. This is not the way I wanted to cut the strings.

G

SAVED BY A FIREMAN

The sounds of sirens fill the air on any given night in Manhattan. New Yorkers are accustomed to finding peace amidst the chaos of city living. For many it brings comfort. It is a cherished lullaby. Detective Cordova had barely 20 minutes of sleep when his landline began to ring at home. He stretched his arm out to reach for the telephone and found a hand full of stubbled face and hair instead. Tony groaned and rolled over, never missing a second of sleep in the movement. His breathing took Danny Cordova right back to where he wanted to be; cuddled together in their Chelsea apartment bed after Tony's 24-hour fireman shift and Danny's ever growing homicide case load in lower Manhattan. They had made love after almost a week apart physically and worlds apart mentally. The stress of being a detective married to a fireman was both crazy bad for their social life and crazy good for them sexually. This was a sleep brought on by both exhaustion and satisfaction, now interrupted.

Danny sat up in bed to his mobile phone Rihanna ring tone blaring. "This better be fucking good." he said to his partner and fellow Detective, Maria Soto. "It's good for the decent people of New York. We have a jumper in our hood." Maria replied. "How is that a reason to call me? I solve homicides. You're killing me. Maybe that's the crime." he laid back down on Tony's chest to end the call and get back to sleep. "You know this jumper Danny, I'm sorry. It's Sonny." Maria waited for questions but instead heard Danny gasp and his feet hit the ground in the back ground. "Where?" he asked. "At the bottom of the Barclays Bank building." "I'm on my way." he said and hung up before she could warn "brace yourself."

Danny Cordova wasn't always the well-dressed detective he is today. He learned his style from being a foot soldier in the very gay mafia controlled fashion industry. His duties fluctuated between helping the models cope with the stress of the business by giving them the infamous Leticia Maldonado "cocktail", an illegal drug mixture that kept them going and calm, and modeling himself. He was often the enforcer, too, when Leticia called on him to hand out a beating. The money was good and so was his exposure to beautiful gay men.

During this time, he lived in a world where he was intoxicated by the power, the sex, and the superficial. It consumed him and although Danny never partook in the party drugs, or even tried the "cocktail" willingly, he remembers the years of working for Leticia as the greatest high ever. It was during this time that he met Sonny. She would make a beautiful man, he often told her, while her conversation was always about getting out of this life.

Sonny had plans and you could not help but be sucked into her dream of a better and decent life. She was as passionate about it as she was feared on the streets. Sonny was the badass that Detective Cordova attributed to his success in the NYPD.

It was Sonny who doctored Danny through a dose of the cocktail that almost killed him when Leticia injected him in a jealous rage.

Leticia laid claim on Antonio Cobian from the minute she saw him modeling Fireman's uniforms on stage. Tony was smart, friendly, sexy, and charming. He was also very innocent and did not know who Leticia was at the time. He flirted with her like any self-respecting fund raiser would. The smile, the hand through his hair, it was all part of his dedication to supporting plastic surgery and pain medication to children injured in fires. He had seen firsthand how helping these children feel less disfigured could pivot their lives. Losing his sister as a child, in a house fire that also claimed his mother's sanity, had turned Tony into the consummate fire fighter. He went directly from high school into training with the FDNY and is still a man on a mission. Much to Leticia's chagrin, this fire fighter was also 100% gay, and beyond modeling for his cause he had set his heart and body on Danny.

"Cordova, the fine cigar I put in my mouth." Tony whispered in Danny's ear on that first night together. He melted the first time they were intimate and every time he considered Tony's eyes trying to tell him the truth about the whole operation. He wanted Tony to know the truth. That he wasn't an up and coming model but rather a street thug, working for Leticia, and now wanting out like Sonny. He tried so many times but Tony was such a good citizen. The kind of guy who would help old people cross the street and who tied his pile of newspapers perfectly for garbage pickup. He was sure this life, his life of crime, would scare Tony away. Their time together became even more clandestine. Not only was it all a secret to Tony but Danny didn't want Leticia to know that a relationship between them was blooming. He didn't know the extent of her infatuation with the handsome Antonio Cobian but he knew she would worry about the leaking of information.

"The whole-body leaks when you start having orgasms with someone." Leticia would say. "Your mouth starts running when your pussy or ass gets wet too." "If your fuck, fucks up my business, you're fucked too. Remember that fuckers."

Leticia is as deeply evil as she is morally shallow. She discouraged relationships if she wasn't in the middle of one herself. This was one of those times. So, it was no surprise when Leticia lost her mind upon walking in on Danny and Tony engaged in a hearty make out session. Danny had missed her numerous calls. Tony had moved in with him that weekend. They had professed their love for one another and closed out the world. Leticia walked in on their bliss and stood there watching, for a while, seething for so many reasons.

"He doesn't know anything." Danny blurted upon Tony excusing himself from the room. "Not yet." Leticia said. "But this looks like a cozy rat's nest you two are making together." She walked around, hard on her stiletto heels, and peering into every box still unpacked in the room. "No, no, I won't do that, Letty. He will never know anything about you. Or about me, completely." He said nervously. Leticia noticed the shake in his voice and reiterated her threat. "Don't fuck up my business or you're fucked." Followed by "I guess I owe you a house warming gift. Come pick it up tonight. We will talk then too." Her air kisses on both sides of his head smelled like scotch, Danny noticed. When did she pick up that habit, he thought to himself?

Tonight's meeting with her might be the right time to schedule his departure. He would evaluate her mood but if all went right, he would set a goodbye date with her, and come home to tell Tony all about his escapades with Ms. Maldonado.

Their meeting that night did not go well. Danny walked into a trap and attack that Leticia must have planned in the short, but rage filled time, after leaving his apartment. Three, maybe four, of her goons beat him to a swollen bloody pulp upon entering her darkened home. He had access through her garage where he always brought in the furs and clothing sent from 7th Avenue as part of her perks for model management, drugs, money laundering, and protection. She kept screaming that someone is breaking in, and help me, all the while considering his eyes filled with horror and tears. Danny Cordova knew to fear Leticia, that it was her way of managing her crews, but he never thought that she would hurt him.

When he came to, she was lying next to him on the floor, a drunken mess and crying. "I didn't know it was you Danny. I swear, I didn't know Papo." His jaw was broken and his left eye was swollen shut. He could not feel his hands and feet but only because Leticia had administered a double dosage of the cocktail to help him with his pain, supposedly. She laid next to his body sobbing until Sonny came running in. "Help him please. Oh, my God, we thought he was breaking in. I gave him medicine for the pain but take him to your place and get a doctor." Through his right, still open eye, he saw Leticia hand Sonny a significant wad of money. "Don't let that fucker die. He has a new lover waiting for him at home." She said.

Leticia bent down and put her full face in front of his one open eye, as Sonny and the goons picked him up to transport him out of her house. No one could see her smile, but Danny did. "Not so handsome now." She whispered. "Leticia is here for you."

She is a sick fuck. These were the first words that Danny wrote down for Sonny and Tony after his ordeal in Leticia's house. Sonny spent the next two weeks helping Danny get past the cocktail alone.

It is an ugly combination of morphine, heroin, cocaine, and amphetamine, "Everything everyone wants, but should not have." as Leticia would say followed by a raucous laugh. The amount given to Danny should have killed him but somehow his body used it to help in the repair process.

Sonny nursed Danny through it all. She took great care of him. She even took care of telling Tony all about Leticia and what was going on. He did not walk out on Danny and instead brokered a deal with Leticia for his release from a life of crime or any indebtedness' to her. He would never disclose the nature of their agreement but Sonny often said that it was a promise not to set Leticia's world on fire without any fire fighter response. Whatever understanding they came to, it was healthy for all.

Sonny and Tony both attended his NYPD graduation years later. And he became a detective quickly thanks to Sonny's sporadic information along with his knowledge of all that goes on. Leticia respected his NYPD position too. Tony's agreement remained a driving factor but she also knew better than to piss off a clean cop of distinction. Detective Daniel Cordova was known for his badassery and heart on the streets. And now he would do everything he could to repay Sonny for saving his life, those many years ago.

Danny made mental notes of everything he would have to handle for her as he drove to the scene. As far as he was concerned it was a crime scene. He could not believe that Sonny would take her own life. They had talked about her life plans and fears, over beers, just last week. Her biggest fear was for her life to end without notice. That no one would care if her death was foul play. That Raya would be left without anything if she died suddenly. These are not the thoughts of someone planning to jump from a rooftop but of someone wanting to live.

G

CONFESSIONS OF A BISEXUAL

Another long night alone at home with the dog was driving Raya crazy. I cannot imagine doing this for much longer, she thought to herself. Her daily routine was slowly becoming an unimaginable rut. Raya had left three voice mail messages in Sonny's inbox already. The first was simply boredom. The second message was coy and flirtatious. By the third call she was annoyed, verging on hysterical, and thinking about calling her ex. Her anxiety, if that is what it was, had truly gotten the best of her tonight.

Raya shuddered at the thought of Sonny hearing those words when listening to the last voice mail message. "I'm not a toy you put away until you're ready to play, Sonny. I am not feeling the love. Call me or I will be finding it elsewhere." Raya said, in anger, and with the intention to sting. It had been several hours since that last call and she now regretted her words. She meant them, every syllable, but voice mail was the wrong delivery system. She should have waited to have this conversation at home. Isn't that what Sonny always said? "Talk to me face to face. Don't write or leave messages. When I am here, I am here completely for you." The fact that Sonny had not returned her call spoke volumes about her anger that Raya had done this again. She is cooling off, and tonight, bedtime conversation will be intense. "Am I just fishing for a break up?" Raya asked Bullet, their Dachshund puppy. "Well, we may break up but I'm not a stay at home dog Mama! Oh, no I'm not, uh uh, you know that don't you puppy boy?" Bullet rolled over for a belly rub, oblivious to the actual words but focused on the tonality of his human Mama.

The truth is Raya had already started to converse with her ex. It began innocently after running into him on a subway station platform. How are you? What's new and exciting? You look great! All the normal questions, answers, and statements that come out of a gaping mouth when you're looking up at the person who rocked your world for a period. She didn't intend to continue the conversation beyond the Canal Street station but he gave her his new number. The nose of the train coming into the opposite platform drowned out what Raya thought was her loud heartbeat. Xavier didn't just hand it to her on any piece of paper either. It was written in the most beautiful penmanship at the top of a page of a poetry book he had in his hand. He was always very bohemian and smooth or 'suavemundo' as we say on the streets. It was just as easy to be lost in his eyes as it was to be fascinated by his mind. Sonny and Xavier could not have been any more opposite. She was rough, honest, exciting and an adventure. Xavier was easy, serene, deep and stable. He made love but Sonny fucked is how Raya once explained the difference. "In a perfect world, I would combine the two to create my perfect person." She would lament. Raya was madly in love with Sonny but not with their life together. The whole 'G' thing was unbelievable in the beginning. It was straight out of a movie with all the thrills. Watching Sonny empty her pockets of large sums of money and put her various weapons away at the end of the night was a turn on. There was such power in her thug touch and attitude. Raya quivered, remembering, and now craving to be touched.

If Sonny doesn't call in the next hour, I will call Xavier. She will probably not come home until tomorrow anyway. The streets are her mistress, Raya thought, growing angry.

Another lonely meltdown was brewing. Raya laid in bed, with Bullet cuddled right beside her, thinking about it all. Thinking about Xavier, his gentle touch, just as the telephone rang. "Sonny, I'm so sorry about my message." She said desperately as she answered the phone quickly. "Please come home. We need to talk."

"It's me Raya, it's Danny, I'm on my way over right now.

G

G

INNER THOUGHTS

"Why haven't I had a damn heart attack?" Sonny thought as she fell to earth, her mind trying to protect her from the reality of her situation. The result looming, but somehow, inexplicably delayed. Unable to move, above and beyond her descent, her mind was working overtime. "Okay, okay, let me try and piece this all together." She thought. "How did this happen?" followed by "Who cares, stupid bitch, you're not going to survive to tell!"

In an instant, Sonny's shirt caught one of those forceful winds created by the tunneling streets and buildings in downtown Manhattan. The top flew up and over her head, exposing her bra and chest. It sounded like a parachute opening and instantly she thought "Maybe I'll survive! Yes, I believe this top has some satin in it. Aren't parachutes made of satin? I could survive this 56-floor plummet! Raya will see that badassery on the news!

It still may hurt." Fear kicked in at the thought of pain and she felt her heartbeat begin to race. "Here comes that heart attack I asked for." The thought that she could survive the fall but die of the scare crossed her mind. "I'm afraid of the pain." She said out loud. Her voice sounded like a bird's tweet under these "flying" conditions. "Pain brought me here." Sonny remembered.

It was only a couple of months into Sonny's relationship with Raya when she woke up unable to move her right arm and her speech slurred. She tried to get dressed and brush it off as the after effect of a bad tequila hangover from the night before, but Raya was worried. By the time they made it over the Verrazano Bridge, into Brooklyn, Sonny was also experiencing tremors. All her symptoms subsided once the tests at Maimonides hospital were concluded but Sonny would receive some very unexpected news two weeks later.

"Your symptoms are indicative of young-onset Parkinson's disease." The doctor said. His words eerily echoed in the hallways of the hospital like background music in a horror film. He spoke of focal dystonia, which is cramping or abnormal posturing of one part of the body. He warned Sonny of pain, dementia, and reactions to the medication he was prescribing. It was all surreal, too quick, and hard to accept. They talked about it and cried together when they returned home. Now more than ever Sonny was determined to leave a life that was not mentally healthy for her. Considering her diagnosis, they put a plan into action and set a date to normalcy.

The levodopa prescribed made Sonny dizzy, nauseous, and caused her muscles to hurt more than normal. It didn't make her line of work easy. For the first time as a G she was often afraid of doing what she did, and she was continuously in pain. She was cranky and her thoughts were scattered, although she did not let on how she was feeling to anyone. Before her diagnosis, Sonny was meticulous, but now she could not think straight. That corny joke that she said so often "I'm so butch, I can't even think straight.", was now a true representation.

"Yes, pain brought me here." Sonny thought, again, fading in and out of consciousness.

Her parachute like top corrected itself in the wind tunnel effect of falling and was now covering her chest again. It was at this moment that she realized her eyes were closed all this time. Sonny struggled to focus on the building as she descended. "What floor have I passed? Who did this? Could Leticia have ordered a hit on me?" Nothing made sense. "How much longer before I hit?" She relaxed her face from the grimace that had now become painful. A sense of peace came over Sonny and she spread her arms out like wings. She was still dropping at a much faster rate than she recognized. "Serenity." Sonny said to herself as she looked up to concentrate on the star filled sky. "Please remember me as the person who wanted more for us, my beautiful Raya." She spoke this out loud and felt her words take flight. "And Leticia, this is when I come for you bitch. Once I hit the ground, you can no longer hurt me. Revenge from another dimension is called Karma. I will haunt you Ms. Maldonado."

G

G

ENTER THE DRAGON

Tall majestic trees line the streets of Todt Hill, an established high income neighbourhood in Staten Island. Of note, it is the highest natural point in the five boroughs of New York City and the highest elevation on the entire Atlantic coastal plain from Florida to Cape Cod.

Leticia Maldonado wanted to own a home in this particular area of New York for as long as she could remember. This was the neighborhood that all her organized crime Johns would return to after an evening with Leticia. That was many years ago but she craved that suburban family life for so long and it drove her real estate choices. More attractive to her than the beautiful home she had found here, finally, was the fact that Todt was the German word for dead.

Leticia Maldonado lived on death hill amongst the Italian mafia families of New York and it was no coincidence.

Stunningly beautiful even before Leticia fully transitioned to become the woman she is today; her early life was spent satisfying many of New York's mobsters on the dark streets of Little Italy. Her golden skin, long beautiful hair, and hour glass figure was just the appetizer. She was smarter, sophisticated, and classier than the typical girls turning tricks back then too. John Gotti himself, the big apple's dapper don, had called Leticia 'a whore you could marry'. And while most of the men seeking her services were on the down low, looking for Gay sex, they never referred to her or treated her like anything less than a lady. 'Blessed by Gotti' would become her moniker and part of the resume that put her in the position of running everything, all organized crime, for the gay mafia.

Still, she resented that while many would court her and fuck her, none ever proposed or professed their love. The pain went deeper than just that. Made to endure countless beatings and ridicule at the hands of her own father simply for expressing herself as female at a very young age, had scarred Leticia. "I grew up unloved. I don't miss what I've never had." She would sadly lament followed by the self-saving "I know they miss me." And while she may have been blessed by a Godfather, none saw her beyond the business. Over the years, this long life of rejection, starting with her family, had embittered her. She held no hopes of settling down with anyone and instead reacted to anybody's romantic bliss with anger and disdain. Her bouts with dysphoria, and hormonal pangs, often made her psychotic. Leticia had been known to kill without any real provocation but could always, somehow, justify it. Those who worked for her feared her. "I pay you to love me but don't ever fuck me if you want to live." That was the best of Leticia's team meeting motivational speeches.

She made a lot of money for the Italians, herself, New York, and the Gay mafia, as a whole. She was revered and respected for that even with the crazy moments that many had to contend with. Those incredible profits allowed her the luxury of her sexual reassignment surgery by some of the best doctors in New York. She chiseled her face, butt, hips, and hands until she was satisfied with the woman she saw in the mirror but she would never achieve the happiness that she thought it would all bring her, sadly.

Leticia was somewhat emotionally attached to anyone who made her money and followed her instructions. She was also attracted to intelligence. "Loyalty from a stupid motherfucker is just a burden but smart people who work for me and stick by me are my children." She was married to the mob, and the business, and these were the children she had always wanted but could not have.

The wine glass fell out of her hand. She was startled by the telephone ringing.

"Thank God my glass was empty." She said without thinking when she answered.

"Excuse me. Its Detective Dan Cordova, Ms. Maldonado."

Leticia: "Look at you all formal and police like. I recognize the fucking voice. What do you need, Detective?"

"I wanted to tell you that we have a homicide that may be connected to you. I'm on my way to the crime scene. This is both a heads up and some questions, if you don't mind."

Leticia: "I'm not connected to any homicide, Dan. You know better than that. And it is late for questions. I need my rest."

"Wait Letty. Its Sonny. Her body is at the bottom of the Barclays Bank building. Was she there for you." Danny heard a gasp before the phone was covered. He could also faintly hear a wail and crying. This was the same woman who cried for him after she attempted to murder him so he was unmoved by her theatrics.

Faintly, Leticia answered "Yes." "She was making my deposit. I would never hurt her Dan, you know that."

Dan Cordova swallowed his own emotion to answer. "I'll make my conclusions after a full and thorough investigation, Ms. Maldonado. Given the nature of your relationship with the victim, that will include many of your projects around the city should be put on hold."

Leticia: "I understand."
"I'll be there in the morning."

Leticia: "I'll have coffee waiting."

"It's not a fucking social call Letty. It's a homicide investigation. Don't go anywhere."

Leticia: "I'll be right here handsome. I have nothing to hide. Espresso. Two sugars. Right?"

Detective Cordova ended the call.

G

G DOWN

The first NYPD officers to arrive to where Sonny's mangled body lay on the street went on to secure the scene immediately.   Homicide Detectives Dan Cordova and Maria Soto arrived separately but quickly. Evidence technicians were in route and the only witness was being questioned ten minutes after he called 911.

Unfortunately, he was a broker who had fallen asleep in his car after an evening of drinking, after work, only to be awakened by the sound of the body hitting the pavement next to him. In shock, but not yet sober, he called the police.

"911, what is your emergency?"

"A body just hit the ground right next to my car." He said, half screaming and half crying. "I think it's a woman. Oh my God, hurry, the body moved. Her legs are moving. I don't know what to do. There is blood and flesh on my windshield. It is everywhere!" He continued.

"Calm down sir. I'm sending someone over right away. In the meantime, I need you to answer a few questions for me. Okay?"

"Yes. Okay." Sobbing. "I'm going to be sick."

911 Operator: "What is your name?"
"Paul Samarco."

911 Operator: "Thank you, Paul. Are you in a safe location?"

"Yes. I think so. Please hurry there is blood everywhere."

911 Operator: "What is your exact location, Paul?"

"I am parked across the street from 10 Barclay Street, downtown Manhattan. I was drinking, I mean I went out and I can't drive." He mumbled. "Yeah, sleeping. And, oh Jesus, she fell from the sky. What is happening?"

911 Operator: "Paul, the police are on their way. I need you to remain calm. Answer my questions. Do you know the woman who fell from the sky?"

"I'm not even sure it's a woman. No, I don't know her. I was sleeping in my car. Her legs are still moving." Paul began to cry and wail. "SHE IS STILL ALIVE!" he yelled hysterically! "Hurry the fuck up!"

911 Operator: "Paul, are you a doctor.?"

"No, no, I'm a broker."

911 Operator: "So you can't make a diagnosis, alright? Paramedics will arrive to do all that they can. Just a few more questions before everyone gets there. Did you witness the accident? Did you see where the body came from or fell from? Can you describe the person in a little more depth for

me? Don't touch anything or get too close, just from where you're standing please."

"I didn't see anything. The sound of the body hitting the ground woke me up. It sounded like an explosion. There is blood and guts everywhere." The 911 dispatcher could hear his sobs and gasps for air.

911 Operator: "You're doing great Paul. Breathe. Thank you for your help. Can you give me a description?"

"I can't see the face. I mean it's bad and I can't make it out. She has on expensive running shoes, blue jeans, and a dressy shirt. It could be women's apparel but the hair and hands look masculine."

911 Operator: "Thank you again, Paul. There is an officer walking over to you now. They are there. Can you see the patrol car?"

"Yes. I can."

911 Operator: "Good, they will take it from here Paul. Is there anything else I can do for you?"

"Can you please call my wife?"

The gravity of what Mr. Samarco was witnessing hit him the hardest just as the officer approached him. He was now completely sober and aware of the human flesh splattered all around him. An ambulance arrived just at that moment too.

"Please don't move sir." The police officer said. Paul Samarco was standing in the middle of a body part explosion and critical evidence.

Both detectives needed to compose themselves. The scene was gruesome and made worse by Dan Cordova's friendship and love for Sonny, now simply known as the deceased. "You really should not be on this case, partner." Maria advised. "You're too close bro. You could make mistakes. We should both consider handing this over to central or the organized crime unit."

Silence.

Dan used a pen to lift the hair from Sonny's face. "Her eyes are still clear." He said, standing up quickly. The tears began streaming down his face. "She was alive on the ground after hitting." Maria was writing. "Yes. Time of death was declared by the EMTs. I'm sorry Dan." She was now looking up at the Barclays Bank building. "Did you hear me Detective Cordova?" "Yes." He answered quickly. "Dropping this investigation isn't an option. I could not save her but I'll be damned if I don't at least give her justice. Who would I be if I abandoned her now, Maria?"

"What do we have from the witness?" Dan struggled to hold it together and remain professional.

"Nothing substantial. He was awakened by the fall. Paul Samarco went out drinking and was sleeping it off in his car."

"Anything on Paul?" Detective Cordova checked.

"Broker. 39 years old. Clean. No criminal record. No parking tickets. Wife and two kids in Long Island. Boring on any day that ends in the letter y. An innocent bystander by all counts. I suspect he is permanently sober after this. He has been vomiting since blue arrived." A chuckle made its way out of her mouth.

"Does that flag pole usually have a flag on it?" Detective Soto pointed up to where there was what appeared to be a battered flag pole at the roof line of the building.

"I'm going to assume yes. And the pole itself looks odd. Let's go up. "Dan Cordova sprinted across the street and into the Barclays Bank lobby with Maria Soto right behind him.

"Every inch of this building is in lockdown for forensics and evidence gathering." He shouted as they entered the elevator. "We may not be able to do that detective." A uniformed officer answered. He was assigned to viewing the building's security footage. "Why not? It's a crime scene."

"In the city that never sleeps, it's a bank building that needs to go about its normal day, come 9:00am detective. That is four hours from now. We don't have the power, or the time to ask someone who does, to shut it down."

"I don't give a flying fuck about power, officer. Wrap your yellow crime tape around this motherfucker and put a closed sign in the door. Anyone who questions that call needs to speak to me or Detective Soto. You got that?"

"Yes sir, I'm just blue for you." He smiled and continued to watch what was recorded that day, from the starters desk in the lobby.

The American flag that once hung on the pole high atop the building was now on the roof in a wrinkled pile. It had been ripped from its cord and the cord removed from the rivets of the flag itself. They bagged both as evidence although it was still not clear how either had been used in this crime.

What was certain was that Sonny did not jump or take her own life. She fought hard to get away and to save her own life. The signs of struggle were everywhere. The scuffed black top was recent and caused by a hard-sole shoe or shoes. Sonny's expensive running shoes were soft Italian leather that would not cause this kind of damage.

Detective Maria Soto began to mark the many blood splatters on the roof too. "Clearly someone took a beating up here." She confirmed what Dan too had concluded. "It was a fucking battle." He said "And she would have been carrying. Look for a weapon Maria."

Maria's flashlight lit up one of the plumbing vents on the vast roof of the building causing something to shine back at her. "Something here!" She shouted. Dan Cordova stood over her as she used her pen, followed by long evidence tweezers, to extract whatever it was. "It's shiny but small." She concentrated on her work.

"What is it?" he asked standing tall above her.

"Hold on." Maria was bagging whatever she had found in the darkness now.

"Did you check Sonny's hands, by chance?"

"For what?"

"For a missing digit?" Maria held up the clear evidence bag to reveal a relatively freshly severed ring finger with a gold wedding band attached."

Dan looked at the finger closely. "She was hard core butch but I know her hands. She cleaned my wounds long enough for me to memorize them. This isn't hers. Nope. Not hers but I can't tell if it is male or female"

"I do know it was not cut off using a weapon." He went on. "It is bitten off! Badass bitch left us clear, concise, evidence of who did this to her. I need to check her mouth before we submit the ring and finger for prints and information."

"She was so tough." Detective Cordova thought to himself, proudly. That feeling quickly dissolved to sadness. How sad that she had to fight so hard without help. His heart hurt at the thought of having to tell Raya all of this. There was so much love between these two women and they had great plans for a decent future.

Sonny often spoke about planting a garden or writing poetry in her spare time. She softened with every item on her new to do list.

"You really plan on retiring to an old lady life, Son?"

"I do. Completely. You can't be a G forever. I want to lengthen my life!" She replied, with that beautiful smile that exposed the deepest dimples.

Now back downstairs, Dan Cordova looked up at the 56-story building one more time. He could not imagine her fall nor the anger or depravity for life that it would have taken to throw her from that roof.

The sun was beginning to rise. The body was starting to smell. "Long day ahead of me." Dan thought. "Long day looking for someone who is short one finger."

G

G

TEARS AND SNOT

Bullet jumped from the bed and ran down the hallway to bark at the door. Raya listened, barely awake, for Sonny's key in the front door and the click of the lock. The dog must have cried and barked for a good five minutes before Raya woke up to the banging. She wrapped the blanket around herself to answer since she always went to bed naked. "Quiet, quiet Bullet. I got it sweetie. Good boy." she said softly followed by "What happened to your keys, baby?" just as she opened the door.

Detectives Dan Cordova and Maria Soto stood in front of her, in the opening, with their heads down. They were both wrinkled and disheveled after a long night on the scene and waiting for the medical examiner to carry the body and parts away. She had promised to begin the autopsy right away as a favor to Dan.

Raya blinked and pulled the blanket around her tighter as a cool morning breeze embraced her. "Hey, what's up?

Hi. Oh man I look terrible. Come in. Come. Damn y'all, its friggin early for me. Sonny isn't home yet. You two look like shit." Raya walked in, towards the kitchen, dragging her blanket behind her. "Seriously, what's going on?"

"When was the last time you spoke with Sonny?" Maria did not hesitate to begin the interrogation. "Café Bustelo, Dan? The last time?" She turned towards Maria. "Last night. I was speaking to her in messenger through the night. Why? Is she being investigated for something?" Raya began to make coffee, filling the pot with water when Dan put his arms around her blanket and all. Startled, Raya turned in his arms to look at him face to face. She saw his tears. She looked frantic and her voice became louder. "NO? WHAT? Is, is Sonny alright? Nooooo, no, no, no!" She repeated "Danny tell me." Raya screamed.

"I'm sorry Raya." Detective Cordova sobbed on Raya's shoulder. "She was murdered last night." Raya's body went limp in his arms. Maria called for an ambulance while Bullet barked uncontrollably at the two visitors.

Raya came to before the paramedics arrived and was sitting up silently on the couch, where Dan had carried her to. Bullet lay next to her scared and concerned for his Mommy. She was stable but they administered a sedative to keep her from going into shock. Raya was shivering. Tears and snot streamed down her face but she did not make a sound.

"I hate to be a jerk, Raya, but I am required to ask you some questions." Raya looked up at Maria as she finished that sentence. Dan shot his partner a dirty look at the same time. "We want to catch the person or persons who did this while the trail is hot. Part of that process is ruling out everything else. And there may be something you remember that will help us."

"I was home after work and some errands." She began to answer. "I spent the night with Bullet, alone with him. The last time I spoke with Sonny she told me she was going to be later than anticipated. Later than most nights. We fought about it or rather Sonny shut down and I sent her unhappy messages through messenger. I didn't kill her and I don't know who killed her. Now get the fuck out of my house and find out who did bitch."

"Easy Raya." Dan interrupted, stepping in between them.

"NO DANNY! she is gone, my baby is gone. I need you two to find out who and why just like she did for you. Quickly!!! She didn't stop to ask questions." Raya was fully screaming and crying as she spoke. "She just jumped in to make sure you didn't die, Danny." "WHO DID THIS?" "How did they kill her?"

Danny put his hands on top of his head. He knew she would ask and dreaded answering.

"Oh God, Raya." He said crying. He dropped to his knees in front of her. "They through her from a roof! 56 stories man." Raya and Dan embraced to wail uncontrollably in unison. "I'm sorry, I'm so sorry." He repeated over and over while holding her in his arms tightly. Just then Bullet howled, as if he knew, that his master and friend was gone.

Detective Maria Soto decided to walk around the house looking for any sign of a connection to Sonny's death while Danny and Raya consoled each other. "I don't believe she is involved but it is my responsibility to rule it out, formally." She thought to herself as she picked up a piece of paper from the night stand.

In print it read;

When you come to me, unbidden,

Beckoning me

To long-ago rooms,

Where memories lie.

The rest of the poem was cut off but the top of the page indicated it was written by Maya Angelou. In blue pen, and in cursive, someone named Xavier had added, Raya I would love for you to call me 917-555-2345. Maria used her evidence tweezers to pick it up and bag it.

G

G

G

INNER THOUGHTS 2 FALL BY

I've decided to embrace the serenity of my impending death. There is a beauty in this fall if you turn off the panic. The fight for life breeds fear. We dread death for only two reasons, fear of the unknown and fear of pain. Shock should mask my pain and I don't believe in heaven or hell, now that I'm nearing the end. Even time has proven to be a falsehood for here I fall in what appears to be slow motion. I can feel and express every emotion. Love is embracing me like a cushion for my fall. The city sleeps as I descend and I can hear it breathing softly. Yes, these are random maybe even abstract thoughts to some, but there really is no need for conversational rules in this situation. It's almost like I am entering the grieving process for myself. I started out surprised, unable to cope with the loss. I entered the angry, swearing, stage. Now I am finding peace with my death. Although, I suppose I will end this life, grieving and missing it all. There certainly isn't another dimension or spiritual plane that could keep me from missing my Raya and all that we planned together.

"Is it too early to pick our wedding invitations?" she asked me at 3 in the morning, just a few months into our relationship. "Yes, I need some sleep now." I replied in jest. We both knew she meant almost a year ahead of our date, which was also just that. We didn't have anything but a date, to be honest, but the love and lust was incredibly powerful. Not just that but also the chemistry. I'll never have that kind of chemistry with anyone again. Okay, that's a brief, insane, but very funny fucking thought. It just occurred to me that insanity is not only acceptable when within seconds of death, but also necessary. Nobody is going to say, she was a damn looney toon just before she hit the ground. Instead they will look for the crazy person that would have me thrown from the roof.

Why was my guard down today? I'm always so careful when making Leticia's deposits. I had counted $446,200 last night before going to bed. To be precise, I had counted it three times. Once at pick up from Letty's house in Staten

Island. "I'm amused that you count my money in front of me after I have told you the amount." Leticia said sarcastically. I never wanted her to accuse me of stealing as she had done to others in the past. Her moods had become more and more erratic and if you let your guard down, she would find an excuse to kick your ass, or rather have someone do so. It was sadistic because she enjoyed creating the drama and watching others suffer as a result. "That's what I'm here for, to amuse you Leticia. And to keep you honest." I answered while wrapping it all in bundles of $10,000. I winked and smiled at her too. "Aye, el Papi chulo de la casa. You're cute Sonny, I'll give you that. Make sure it all makes it safely to its destination, darling." I remember thinking she must be tired. No word joust?

Back to counting. So, I counted it upon receipt, I counted it before I went to bed, and counted it for the third and last time before I left the house with it bagged.

I drove to the bank building just as I did every week. The deposit isn't done at a teller's window or even in the bank at all, that I know of. My responsibility is to deliver the cash to someone waiting for me on the roof. Quietly, unassumingly, no fuss and no mess. The building starters, either Germaine or Johnny Irish, depending on the day, knew me. They knew to let me in and up, in exchange for a very generous tip. This tip also purchased their loyalty and silence. It was, after all, an additional $30,000 a year for their families. I made it upstairs without issue. Nothing felt wrong or out of place. The Italianos waiting for me on the roof top counted the money and left. At least I thought they did. I always wait until I watch them leave the building before I take off.

More pee running down my leg! Why is my body dehydrating me before I hit the ground? Is it some sort of biologically connected OCD in an effort to make less of a mess? I truly hope no one is looking up, but back to my recollection of events.

I was looking over the short rooftop wall, watching for them to leave before I headed to the elevator, when someone suddenly draped material over my head and tried to choke me to death at the same time. It was the buildings fucking American flag! No please don't kill me with the stars and stripes, I thought, thinking what a funny story I will tell when I survive this shit. I could see the shoes. It's not the Italianos trying to scare me or worse, kill me. Theses shoes are not meticulously polished Italian leather footwear master pieces. These are black working shoes. They are on the feet on someone who was paid to take me out. Paid by who, is the question? Leticia Maldonado is the only person I know that can order a hit for no reason but that you're too damn happy for her liking.

And yet, even this was too easy and unnecessary for her. I fought as hard as I could but I guess either the weakness caused by my Parkinson's', or the medication itself, was a hindrance. That's my excuse and I'm sticking to it. My last thoughts should not be of me second guessing how badass I truly am.

I almost made it to the door when they dragged me back like Betsy Ross trapped in her own creation. Flag and all, I felt them lift me over the wall. "Motherfucker!" was my last word before my feet left the ground and it felt good to say. I highly recommend it for anyone who is being murdered. They held onto the flag just before I hit the air to free fall. I looked right at their patriotic Motherfucking faces.

G

PULL MY FINGER

Of all the forensic evidence collected at the Barclays Bank rooftop the severed finger was most promising. Not only would the bite marks that severed the finger be of importance, but the fingerprint identification itself was imperative.

Detective Soto had documented the crime scene thoroughly including 400 or so pictures, the labeling of over 200 paper evidence bags, and 72 plastic bags containing plaster casts of impression evidence. The roof gravel was soft enough that even the shallowest of steps, and the many that were indicative of a fight, had produced lab worthy prints for evaluation. She had also found many broken fingernails, all bagged, in the hopes that the striations could determine how many people were on the roof, besides the victim. Forensic science can date the nail clippings and all fingernail striations are unique, much like bullet striations.

"I need the body checked for trauma, blood and seminal fluid." Maria added. "Do we suspect sexual assault or rape, detective?" the lab technician asked. "I'm not ruling anything out. Whoever did this was vicious. We must rule this out as a hate crime and she is a lesbian. Was a lesbian" she fumbled with her words. "I'm going to hope not." She continued. "Also, can you get an impression of her fancy sneakers? I pulled up a lot of prints on that roof."

Danny tossed and turned for the mere two hours that he could sleep before jumping out of bed and into the shower. He placed his forehead on the cold tile to try and numb his headache. His eyes were swollen from all the crying. "Why would someone kill her?" he had wailed, while engulfed in Tony's muscular arms. He had held it in, for the most part, while at the crime scene helping Maria collect evidence. The hole he felt in his chest was overwhelming. It took his breath away. It kept him up for most of the short night. Tony was so nurturing, and so loving, but had to leave him for this weeks' twenty-four-hour shift. "Babe, I'm sorry, I wish I could stay." He leaned down to kiss Danny goodnight. "If you need anything, call me." Tony Cobian left for his station and long shift as a firefighter.

"Review the key facts of this case." Danny thought to himself while battling with his tie in front of the mirror.

Documentation. "I have a secondary witness and many pictures to review in the murder book, so far." "I need the forensic reports from Maria." He thought about the finger. It appeared to be chewed off. It was consistent with the timeline, freshly done. "Who does it belong to?" "Fingerprints? Saliva?" he made a mental note.

Timeline. "Witness stated that the body fell next to his car at 1:10am." Detective Cordova was still itemizing the investigation to himself as he unlocked his NYPD issued weapons out of his nightstand gun vault. "How long was she on that roof." He wrote in his Murder Notebook 1. Question building starters, Germaine and Johnny Irish and 2. Need Officers notes "What was on the building tapes?"

Follow every lead. "This was an execution style death. I have to examine who has a motive." No case in Detective Dan Cordova's professional career was more important than bringing Sonny killer to justice. It is either not as straight forward as anyone would think or incredibly simple. "The obvious are Leticia Maldonado or Raya." His mind flashed back to Raya's reaction last night and what appeared to be such pain. More notes; 1. Sonny and Raya's bank account statements and activity. 2. Question Leticia. Examine the many possible motives.

Everything is evidence. "I can't stop thinking about that flag." Danny started his car and stared at the American flag hanging high atop his building for the very first time. "She was still alive when she hit the ground. What did the use it for?" The thought that it didn't belong at all also crossed the detectives mind. "First order of business is to determine what isn't a part of the crime at all."

Persevere. These first 48 hours are critical. "Time to visit with Letty" as he called her. Dan Cordova pulled out of his expensive Chelsea, Manhattan, parking space and headed to the Brooklyn Battery Tunnel.

The traffic towards Staten Island after 9:00am in the morning would give him time to check with Maria and to plan his questioning. Leticia was extremely intelligent and had honed her talent to deceive over many years. To catch her for any murder could be the end to the lucrative racketeering enterprise she had built for herself. It was this bit of knowledge, and Danny's experience with the inner workings of Letty's business, that made her less of a suspect. Detective Soto disagreed. "She is the obvious fucking murderer, Danny!" she argued "She hates for anyone to be happy or in love, she doesn't have to dirty her hands, and she has the money to pay for pros. And whoever threw Sonny from that roof knew she would be there. Let's narrow the list with just that information."

"I'm not so convinced but I'm on my way to her place now. Meet me there, Maria. "

Leticia opened the door as if she was expecting the two detectives for breakfast. "Good morning, handsome. And you too homely, I mean homey." She laughed. She had flung the door open for them both to enter and follow her, assumedly. Her satin robe was exotic and dramatic, the length exaggerated, and it flowed behind her like a wedding dress train. It was purple and majestic giving her the evil queen persona that Danny fully expected. "Have a seat. Can I offer you café Bustelo? I cleared my schedule for this boring visit but let's make the most of it, Detectives." Leticia's snide greeting infuriated Danny. "Sonny is dead. I don't give a fuck how bored you are with this questioning. And were not here to socialize, Letty."

"Aye Papi, why so harsh? Don't get your scrotum all twisted. I'm grieving my baby too." Her voice cracked with emotion as she sat on the gold velvet love seat. She reached for her coffee cup on the table in front of her and pointed for them to sit on the couch. Detective Soto reached into her case file and put several gruesome pictures of the victim on the same table, carefully lining them up in front of Leticia. "Miss Maldonado, this body has been identified as that of Sonny Rojas. Do you recognize her in these photographs? She was killed, thrown from the 56th floor roof top of the Barclays Bank building in lower Manhattan. I understand that she was completing a business errand for you. Is that correct?" Maria Soto waited for her response.   Danny watched for any tell of Leticia's involvement. The room stood still for longer than expected before Leticia Maldonado screamed. "Oh God No, I didn't have anything to do with this." What appeared to be genuine tears streamed from her face as she continued. "She made my drop. She always did and she was meticulous about it. "She sobbed into her hands. "Take these pictures away. Please Danny. You believe me, don't you?"   She looked up at him, her eyes pleading for an answer. "I'm investigating the murder of my friend. The same friend who took care of me after you had me beaten to near death in this very garage." He leaned down close to her face enraged. Detective Soto stood up, instinctively reached for her firearm. "Danny, we need to continue with our questions and Ms. Maldonado has not answered directly. Stand down detective." He grabbed a handful of Leticia's' hair. "Answer the fucking questions and stop the dramatics. You're incapable of love or loyalty. Stop the bullshit." He pushed her head in front of the most horrible picture of Sonny, specifically taken to document what the coroner called the final blow. It showed her neck bones, the cervical vertebrae, broken and piercing through her skin right below her head. "Is this your errand girl, Sonny, who has worked for you since she was 16 years old?"

Leticia's head snapped hard at his release and push towards the table and pictures. "Yes." She said meekly and crying. "When was the last time you saw Sonny." Detective Soto took over again. Her voice was low, soft, like a child being reprimanded and scared. "She picked up the money four hours before delivery."

"What time was delivery, Leticia?" Danny was writing in his murder book as he stood above her, every vein in his neck and head evidence of his pain and anger.

"Delivery is always at midnight. The time can never be changed. They come, they count it, and they leave. It has not changed for the past five years."

She was now drying her eyes and composed. Maria Soto had put the pictures back in her manila file folder. "How much was Sonny depositing for you?" Danny continued. "$446,200, she counted it in front of me. That was her way, thorough. And it was delivered without issue. The bankers confirmed that it was all done and they were in their car in half an hour. It went as it always does."

"I am going to need their names, Letty. "Danny sat next to her. She was disheveled now. Her hair messy after his grabbing her. He noticed how beautiful she is. In this second in time, she looked vulnerable too, but her reminded himself of what a dangerous woman Letty really was.

"You're crazy Papi, I can't give you their names or any information about them. For one, they would kill us if I did and the other reason is they change with every deposit I make. They are smarter than the NYPD." She was regaining her sass. "So, I really don't know." She finished while gathering her long beautiful mane into a ponytail.

He leaned in and put his arm around her to her surprise. She flinched. A sign that he had frightened her. "I'm sorry Letty but you're going to have to give up some information. Not right now. We will give you time to think about it. You have a lot going on in your garage and various warehouses around the city. I'm aware of them all. Your DEA friends are nervous about this murder. I know who they are too and names could end up in Detective Soto's reports. That's how she rolls, my partner is so thorough with the paperwork." He looked at Maria and winked. "They can't protect you when you need them the most if they have to worry about being named."

Both detectives gathered themselves to leave when Danny turned around to say one more thing. "I won't rest until I catch Sonny's killer, Letty, so if you know anything or can help with the investigation I would greatly appreciate it. And if you had anything to do with it." He paused and looked at her directly just inches from her face. "I will take down everything you have built throughout the years. Along with everything you love!"

"We had such a nice visit." Leticia Maldonado was now composing herself. She approached the door as she was speaking. "I didn't kill my best G, Danny. You were useless, disposable, and it was easy to beat your ass, but she was critical to my work. Whoever took Sonny out, hurt my business, so I'm both sad about it and pissed off too. I'm not going to damage my business relationships to help you or the NYPD feel good about yourselves. I will take care of whoever has done this myself. "

Detective Maria Soto turned to speak to Leticia "Don't make matters worse for yourself, Miss Maldonado. This case needs to be handled by law enforcement professionals."

"So polite this one, Danny." Leticia quickly spoke up. "Plain, not easy on the eyes, but impeccable manners." She opened the door. "Give my love to your gorgeous firefighter husband, Cordova. I miss speaking with him. What was our last conversation? Refresh my memory. I'm sure it was about you. It's always about you, isn't it?" She straightened his tie before saying "We may need to catch up, him and I." That wicked laugh that made Danny's skin crawl followed. "Aye dios mio, look at the time." There was no watch or clock consulted. "You both need to get the fuck out of my house."

Danny and Maria walked out of the house and sat in one car to review their notes and to determine their next step. Leticia watched them out of her window while thinking about hers.

"What do we have, Maria? The timeline is that she arrived in the building sometime before midnight since the drop off was at midnight."

"Correct." She answered, "And at 1:10am she hit the ground." Danny felt a pain in his chest hearing it said so matter of factly.

"That's an hour plus. If they were done with the transaction in thirty minutes, there was a lot of fight to get her up and over the roof perimeter." He was thinking. "Talk to me Sonny." He said to himself. "I want the building people in front of us, Germaine and Johnny Irish, bring them in. I also need the building security footage."

Maria opened her file "According to the first blue on scene, Officer Bowen, any footage after midnight has been compromised. We do have Sonny entering and two male individuals entering. I have them trying to identify the two men back at the labs. For now, all we know is approximately six feet tall, both, and one heavier than the other. Ages, somewhere between forty and fifty."

Danny was staring at the house. Leticia was staring back. "What about the finger? Anything?"

Detective Soto was checking her phone and emails. "Left hand, ring finger. Male. Caucasian. It was a fresh sever when we found it. Bitten off. There is one incisor marked clearly but that does nothing for us. Most importantly, the saliva does not match Sonny's.

"What?" Danny snapped out of his stare down trance with Leticia to look at Maria. "Someone else was up there? We know Sonny was there plus two goons picking up the deposit, and possibly others?"

He looked back at the window to see Leticia gone.

Maria concluded

"We know Sonny did not bite that finger off. We need to find out who that finger belongs to. If it belongs to one of the two who picked up the deposit, who else was on the roof, or is one of them the biter? Why? And if neither of them are missing a digit, who else was up there?"

Danny unlocked the car door to leave. "Meet you back at the precinct. Get the building guys in front of me, please. And I want to start swabbing everyone for a DNA match with the biter."

He continued "Leticia, Germaine, Johnny Irish, and even Raya."

Maria was shocked "RAYA? I mean I know technically she will remain a suspect until we have proven her not to be, but really?"

"Everyone! And concentrate on identifying the goons too. I want them in front of me. I want to see their hands."

G

G

G

DESCENSION

I want to speak to Danny before I leave this earth. Alright higher power of religion, folklore, and human creation; how do I turn on my telepathic power? We should all be able to do that in a time of danger or desperation. No wonder we are reactive instead of proactive as a species. We are a design flaw. The body goes into shock to protect you from pain, supposedly, and after the fact, but it would be so much better if you could download to another human being, telepathically, before you go. If I could just say, I'm falling to my death but I wanted you to know that I love you before I die. I could send a message to Raya saying there is some money in the floor in my closet. I could share all of tonight's smells, sounds, and pictures, saved in my head, for Danny to solve my murder case. He would be an NYPD star right away, instead of facing this conundrum.

Can you hear me Detective Cordova? I have some information for you! Did I shout that or am I yelling into my own head? I'm drooling, and it is all over my face, so I know that I opened my mouth. When you say things out loud the universe conspires to make it happen. I read that shit on Facebook.

Take note Danny, if you can hear me. They were all there before me. There were at least four men, two Italianos, and I never saw the others faces. I did see their shoes though. They were dirty working shoes, black. Big feet too. One of them put his hand over the flag that was already over my head. He covered my nose and mouth. I took a deep breath and I could smell barbeque on his hands, Danny, no bullshit. Can you hear me? Barbeque! They were strong but I did head butt one of them hard. Look for the bruise, bruh. And the flag, that fucking American dirty, dusty, flag was on my face. My hair and spit should be all over it. I recognized the Italianos too, although I don't think they would jeopardize their weekly deposit from Leticia's most trustworthy G. Louie and Gino are their first names. I don't know their last names. They are brothers who get their kicks double fucking Leticia. You heard me right. I mean together, like a threesome thing, and they even do each other. How do I know this juicy piece of information? Leticia wanted me and I flirted. This was before Raya, Danny. I mean she is so damn beautiful if you can get past her being evil. Anyway, we used to have our 'late night' cognac after business. I would get lost in her almond shaped eyes, perfect lips, and exotic beauty. Yes, I kissed her several times, and the kisses did get passionate. That hot velvet couch that made me sweat uncomfortably always ruined the mood and brought me back to reality. That was our thing before Raya came along, giving Leticia the affection she craved, and imagining myself strapping on to fuck her hard and painfully. We wanted each other for different reasons, mine was in retaliation for so many things and Leticia really wants to love and be loved. She invited me to watch her with Louie and Gino, one night, and unbeknownst to them. I was hiding in her closet, high on ecstasy, and mesmerized by her sexual prowess. She was fully transitioned to have all my favorite body parts by this time. It was mesmerizing and every so often she would glance at me. Then it got freaky with the brothers doing each other, just as my high was wearing off. I became disgusted with myself and where this relationship with Leticia was going. We had crossed the line. I excused myself from work by telling her I was ill. "Full of snot and germs", I said, to keep her away completely. The truth is I was in hiding. Thinking about my life, what I did for a living, and how I had fully descended into a world of depravity.

I marched over to Letty's house, when the week was over, and said those exact words to her. "You're descending?" she laughed. "Like falling off a roof?" True story, Danny. I remember she said these exact words!

Raya came along after that and Leticia knew I had fallen in love. She could see it but one night she asked me, but in her typical mob boss threatening way. "Does your new-found love create a problem for my business, Puta?" She had now taken to calling me whore. "No Letty, my life outside of your business is none of your business." I answered like a badass. "That's where you're wrong, we merged lives when we became responsible for each other eating." "That makes us family, Puta!" She laughed and ran her hands through my hair. We looked in each other deeply. Mine was a look of pity, laced with fear, and hers was a combination of want and loathing. I remember thinking that she is what not being loved looks like. It's not loneliness, or even horniness, for Leticia could literally have anyone she wanted. She was beautiful, intelligent, and has money. It is purely that love does not grow where there is so much evil and hate lurking and vice versa.

I hope these telepathic memories and thoughts reach you Detective Cordova, my friend and brother from another mother. It is not going to be easy to decipher but I have given you a lot of information. Let us recap because I have nothing to do but fall.

Leticia wanted me and I dumped her. We both know that she has harmed or killed people in the past for simply finding their happiness. She is a love craving bitch but you already know that.

The Italianos are brothers named Louie and Gino. They enjoy threesomes with Leticia and incest with each other.

They have been picking up the deposits lately. They are well dressed, atypical goons, and they live in Staten Island.

The motherfuckers who draped me in an American flag and threw me from the roof of the Barclays Bank building were wearing black work shoes. They had big feet and were strong. One of them should have a bruise on his face from my well-placed head butt. And one of them, might be the same guy, smells like barbeque. It's a strong smell on his hands like he is a cook and immersed in it.

My head is pounding. I must be dehydrated from the loss of body fluids that I am completely releasing during this long, slow, fall.   Please let this be signs of the stroke I will experience before hitting the ground. One of those pain and horror protection ploys in our design, no doubt. Hmm, not so flawed now that I need it to work for me.

I cannot look down to see how much longer before I hit the ground. If this impending death telepathic channel is real, I must connect with Raya quickly. I cannot see how much time I have although time isn't making much sense right now. Everything is still in slow motion. I won't take a chance, there are things she must know before I am gone. I never told her about Leticia and me. I mean, we never had sex but we came damn close to it. It was before her and I happened, but she would be disturbed. For one, she would know that that made me a target for Letty's wrath. It would worry her. Raya, can you hear me? Again, I didn't hear myself but I know I opened my mouth. More drool all over my face. Raya, I love you unconditionally. I know you had reconnected with Xavier. The house has cameras baby. Little tiny ones that are placed in every room. They record to the cloud and I can see them and store them on my smart phone. You need to know that these were installed before you moved in with me and not to watch you but to protect me. Like I said, there is money under the floor boards in my closet. I've been saving my cash for quite a while. You know how much I have wanted out of this life. Even more so after starting a life with you and then receiving that horrible diagnosis. Please don't get angry with me after I am gone. Don't think the worst of me when you get this message, or find it all.

I know it is crazy to think that Danny or Raya can hear me but I have read all about our being made of stardust and our universal connection. There must be some validity to frequency connections.

Where was I? Still falling slowly. Oh yes, Raya I'm sorry but I listened in on every single one of your conversations with X. I know that although you're attracted to him, I rock your world. You didn't say that but I could tell. He keeps you company while I'm running around the city and now, getting myself killed. I fully admit that this is a hard life for anyone waiting for me at home. And now, your most talked about fear has happened. I didn't see it coming, Raya. I'm so sorry. Promise me three things, beautiful.

Number one, that you will always stay close to Danny. He is a good friend, a good cop, and he will protect you.

Number two, that you will pursue a life with Xavier, even if just temporarily after my death. He seems gentle and loving towards you. I need you to try and be happy with him. Maybe for a time through your grief. Whatever you do, be honest with him.

Number three, that you will keep Bullet and take care of him. You're the only Mommy he knows. I'm going to miss our naughty fur baby boy.

When you finally find the money that I hid, as well as see our bank account, I hope you do something wonderful with your wealth. You know babe, the things we spoke about doing together. The many trips we planned and that little cottage that we wanted, on a beach somewhere. You like Cape Cod or Martha's Vineyard. I always wanted it somewhere hot like Puerto Vallarta or Puerto Rico. Whichever place you pick, I will be right there with you, keeping you safe.

Stay away from Leticia. I don't know if she is responsible for my death. Part of me thinks, why would she bring this attention on herself? This is one of those 'obstacles to her success' that she was so against. I also know that Letty's mood swings were deadly and she hated to see other people, especially those close to her, happy and in love. And if I have not said it before Raya, please know that you are the love of my life.

I disconnect from my telepathic umbilical to Raya. I am just trying to piece it all together. My murder was planned. The men who attacked me were in waiting, hiding on the roof. They watched the entire transaction between me and the fuck brothers. That's premeditated right there, Detective Cordova. Sheesh, I can't open my mouth without spit, a lot of it, flowing up into my nostrils and all over my face. I could drown myself! I am going to be such a wet mess when I hit the pavement.

Back to solving my death. Germaine or Johnny Irish must have let them up. Why would they choose to end their supplemental income? Did four men go up to the roof before I arrived? Did Louie and Gino know? Were they a part of it? And the biggest question of all is, did Leticia arrange it all?

If she did, it was the perfect blindside. I'm emotional just thinking about it but there is no possible way that I can cry after the amount of liquid that my body has expelled during this fall. She never showed any sign of unusual anger towards me. To the contrary, we laughed, we worked, and she told me often that I was her best. More than that Letty looked at me with love. It made me uncomfortable. "You're very cute." She said it often. She would tussle my hair and smile at me. I'm not delusional enough to think that Leticia Maldonado, blessed by the Don John Gotti himself, could ever truly love someone. No. She was hardcore deadly bitch; however, she did show me affection. It was subtle and never enough to stop our work. The business of drugs, money laundering, prostitution, and fashion never stopped in the city that never sleeps. There was always something to do, someone to see, or someone to hurt or kill. Hard to believe it was me this time. If she planned it, it was masterful, I'll give her that. I didn't have a clue. The last time that Letty was in any kind of a dangerous mood, or angry at me, was when she gave Danny a beating. That was many years ago and I was more of a danger to her because of it. Truth be told, I thought about killing her, back then, and for what she had done to him. I was so angry I wanted to put a bullet between her eyes. I didn't think I could ever forgive her for what she did to Danny but he healed, not just physically but his whole life. The best revenge or retaliation was Leticia seeing Danny become a legit law enforcement officer and moving up quickly through the ranks to become a detective. I leaked to him constantly, I won't lie, so he could achieve his goals. We shoved his success in her face. And the cherry on this karma dessert was his marriage to Tony. The wedding was beautiful. Letty was gracious but those of us who knew her could see her seething under her makeup. It took days upon days to convince the two of them to invite her. It was for two reasons; one was safety, if she was there then she wasn't home planning how to trash the wedding. Instead, she was consumed with turning heads upon her entrance. She did not disappoint us. Breathtaking is an understatement when describing how she looked on that day.

The second reason was just serving her that dessert I spoke about. Leticia prided herself on being a lady at all times, especially in public. She had practiced her composure, etiquette, and vocabulary for many years when she was tormented by her father for questioning her assigned gender. She connected with Grace Kelly and dedicated her every waking moment to being that woman and a mob boss, at the very same time. We knew that on top of a very generous wedding gift, equal to what she believed was the value of beautiful Tony Cobian and in amends for what she did to Danny, she would also behave impeccably. She was also honored to be invited. It was all a very twisted and contrived wedding invitation. I considered it my crowning achievement, Danny's legit path out of this abbreviated life as well as her attending the wedding.

I'll be even more honest since I am dying, I was jealous of Letty's attraction to Tony. He took her focus off me for a time. And while I was falling madly in love with Raya, I still missed our flirtation. The sexy and coy looks. The innuendos. Her touch, discreet but always there. We all matured into the various relationships we are today and not once did I see or feel anything that would hint towards my being killed today. Not just murdered but planned and vicious. It smells of Leticia, yet doesn't make sense.

I can only hope that my telepathic messages reached their targets, and that even if they don't come in loud and clear, they still lead my loved ones to my killers.

G

G

DREAM CATCHER

The sun shone brightly through the curtains and onto Raya's face as she slept on the couch with Bullet. She confused this warmth for Sonny's kisses on her face. She slept deeply after being sedated by the paramedics. Raya cried in her sleep for twenty-four hours after Danny had given her the horrible news, news that shattered her world. She was now in a deep dream state, speaking with her love. An empty bottle of wine alongside an empty glass was on the coffee table. The notepad where she was writing down what to do next was riddled with tear stains. Bullet was cuddled deep into her stomach and chest. He had relieved himself on the rug in front of the tub in their bathroom but now his stomach was growling with hunger. He waited patiently, focused on her breathing, ready to capitalize on any stirring. He could feel her sadness. Something life changing had happened and Bullet instinctively knew to be consoling, but he was growing hungrier. A low whine made its way out of his throat as he smelled food on her breath.

Raya was locked in her dream conversation. Bullet made his hunger known by putting his paw on her face. It startled her and she opened her eyes. The sun on her face was no longer warm kisses but a piercing pain that felt like someone was stabbing her between her eyes straight to the back of her head and impaling her on the couch. She moaned, signaling Bullet to lick her wound, wherever it may be, beginning with her face and eyes. It felt good and she laid there allowing it to happen.

After fifteen seconds of a face washing by her fur baby along with his unbridled excitement for breakfast, Raya crawled off the couch. She made it to the kitchen and prepared Bullet's meal like she had so many times before. No thinking was required, the dog plate was washed in the drainer, fill the water dish, two scoops of kibble, count to three and serve. Bullet was ravenous and the sound of him eating brought her back to reality. "I can't cry anymore." She said, to no one in particular, but Bullet paid close attention to her every word. "At least not today. I have too much to do. I will handle her funeral arrangements." Sonny did not have any family to reach out to or find. She had told Raya on one of her first dates that she considered herself an orphan. Her childhood was a nightmare. Sonny had survived years of abuse from her heroin and crack addicted parents and she was raised in and out of many foster homes, when the authorities became involved. Foster homes that met the very bare minimum of childcare simply to pass inspections that kept their monthly checks coming. She vaguely remembered an older brother who was whisked away by a caseworker when the abandoned building they were squatting in was set on fire. The man that Sonny believed to be her father died of smoke inhalation, her brother was rescued, possibly adopted by the case worker, and children's services let Sonny remain with her mother in a family rehab facility. The facility rehabilitated very few people who passed through its doors. Instead, Sonny watched as her mother was raped repeatedly in front of her as a child. They ran out on a cold winter night when one of the rapists, an employee of the facility, turned his attention on to five-year-old Sonny. It was the only memory she had of her mother ever protecting her, she would often say, "my ounce of love growing up". Sonny would find herself in the foster system shortly after that when police raided the crack house they had found shelter in. By that time, Sonny's mother was HIV positive with an addiction to anything that numbed her pain, including men. "There was no longer any light in her eyes but I remember her waving goodbye and her toothless smile." They would never see each other again. Sonny became a ward of the court and transitioned from her last foster home to a G on the street simply to survive life.

Invites, Raya wrote down the names of who would attend her loves funeral:

Danny

Tony

Maria

Raya

Letty

She added Bullet's name. "Nothing is sadder than losing someone but the realization that very few will mourn such a loving person." She thought. "I hope that they let Bullet attend. His love is as pure and unconditional as hers always was."

The arrangements proved easier to accomplish than Raya had anticipated. She planned everything through Ortiz Funeral Home in Brooklyn. Sonny called it the funeral home where all G's pass from this dimension to the next. They would coordinate with the medical examiner's office directly and save her the emotional discomfort. There would be no religious send off to a heaven that Sonny did not believe in. Instead, a beautiful urn containing her ashes would rest on a table for twenty-four hours so that a few people and Sonny's beloved fur baby could pay their respects. To Raya's amazement, everything had been paid for and chosen in advance. Sonny would often mention this to Raya but it was never a good time to talk about death. Raya would change the subject, make jokes, and the conversation with end with Sonny reiterating "Okay, but if anything ever happens to me call Ortiz Funeral home in Brooklyn, contact the bank, and look through my closet."

"Bank appointment set, Papi." Raya said to Bullet. He followed her everywhere. "My tail has a tail." As Sonny would say. "Now let's check her closet." "And you thought

I wasn't paying attention." She giggled to herself while looking at Sonny's picture on the mantel.

Raya and Bullet both entered Sonny's beloved treasure trove of stuff, namely "The closet", putting everything on the bed as they sifted through it together.   Bullet was proving himself to be quite the hound dog, sniffing every box, pocket, envelope and corner of the space. Raya followed his 'sniff' hoping to find whatever Sonny thought was so important for her to have after her death, but found nothing right away.   Everything was of value to Raya because it had Sonny's smell or because it was something that had a memory attached to it but why was it important to the list of things for Raya to do, should anything happen?

All her clothes were now on the bed. Her smell filled the room. Raya and Bullet both jumped on the pile to inhale her.   Raya began to cry again, remembering the first time she knew she was falling in love.

They were in this house, Sonny had left to do her thing, and Raya picked up her t shirt, thrown on a chair in the bedroom instead of the hamper. She sniffed it to confirm that it was laundry and instead found herself overcome with emotion and craving to hold Sonny in her arms. "Can you come back home for lunch?" she asked. She had immediately run to the telephone to call her. "Sure, babe, is something wrong?" Sonny asked "Everything is right Sonny, I know I've already told you that I have fallen in love with you but I don't think you know how much. I really need to see you. I'm craving you."

Sonny came home and they made love for hours. It was wild, passionate, on the floor, in every doorway, and eventually on this very bed.

Now looking up from laying on her back in their bed Raya whispered "I will never forget you Sonny, I will never forget your smell or your love. Thank you, baby."

Bullet jumped off the bed and back into the closet. Raya didn't notice how excited he was getting right away but sat up when the scratching became incessant. "Get out of there, what are you doing? I can't deal with bad boy today. Don't make Mommy angry." She was on her feet, pulled out of that wonderful memory of making love, when she reached the closet and saw the ever so slight wider gap between the floor boards. Bullet had his nose in between that tiny gap and was whining as if to say, I found it Mama. Raya kneeled and tried to separate and lift the board, to no avail. Suddenly, she remembered the flat head screw driver on the top shelf. It was odd to find one of Sonny's tools out of place. She was so meticulous about everything being in its place.

The screwdriver fit perfectly in between the boards and lifted the entire closet floor up in one piece. The boards had been joined and hinged to create a door to a deep drawer filled with things that Raya had never seen before.

Right on top was a typed note from Sonny, and it read:

Raya was shocked that for one, Sonny was so thorough and two, that she had gone to such lengths to insure Raya's future. She had even prepared paperwork for Bullet to travel and kept it up to date. These were the abnormally long walks she took with the dog. I always accused her of flirting, or worse, in the dog park. She shoved everything

---

If you're reading this note something has happened to me. Please know that I am always with you now. The following is imperative and meant to protect you if I did not go naturally. I love you Raya, forever and a day, Sonny.

There is a Spanish passport and new identity for you to get anywhere in the world with. Take Xavier and Bullet on a trip. Get away and build a new life. Drive out of New York and into Canada. Buy your tickets in Canada.

There are 52 bundles of $10,000 in US cash. Unmarked and good to use anywhere in the world. You'll have to hide them in the car.

Lastly, the credit card is in your new name and pre-loaded with another $30,000 US dollars. The PIN is that wedding date we always talked about but didn't get a chance to celebrate. Now you can. Please buy any tickets using the

back into the floor drawer and closed the cover. The screwdriver was tucked into one of Sonny's many suit jackets, in the inside pocket. Boxes of shoes, her sports cap collection, and clothes were all returned to place so that they would cover up the access.

She was now nervous, checking everything around her, and shutting the curtains, all in a paranoid frenzy. "I need a shower." She said to Bullet. He wagged his tail and went straight to the bathroom understanding her words. "Good boy." Any other day, she would have celebrated his genius with fanfare and treats, but today she needed to think and calm down. "Yes, a shower and I need to call Xavier." She looked up. A gentle breeze blew over her face. There were no windows open. And then she heard it clear as day "Start a new life, Raya." She thought her mind was playing tricks on her but as she looked down to get ready to shower, there was Bullet staring into space and wagging his tail.

G

G

PRAYING FOR THE TRUTH

Detectives Danny Cordova and Maria Soto made themselves comfortable in what is the NYPD Detective Bureaus Forensic Investigation Unit. This was no longer about Danny investigating the murder of his much-loved friend, but also an organized crime case. With so much evidence to pour through, and the various units that would help them, this was a central location. It was key to solving the case quickly too. They set up a desk and all their paperwork just a few feet from the bath rooms, for convenience, and because they were guests there. The last thing either of them wanted was to get in the way however they needed direct access to CSU. The Crime Scene Unit is responsible for forensic investigations of homicides. Danny and Maria needed their assistance in the processing of the crime scene as well as determining the proper routing of evidence between the Medical Examiner's office, the NYPD Police Lab and the NYPD Property Clerk. The administration of all of this becomes more complicated as the Detectives identified leads.

"I'm sure these two idiots know something." Danny stated as he prepared to question Germaine and Johnny Irish, the security and reception staff on premise when Sonny was killed. "At least half of that statement is true, Cordova." Maria answered. "Germaine is in A1 and Johnny is across the hall in A6. Who are you starting with?"

Germaine sat nervously awaiting someone to open the door to the small room they had sat her in. The room was entirely made of metal, cold and unwelcoming, with a mirror that added to her anxiety level, because it was clearly a one-way glass. She saw them escort Johnny into the room directly across the hall. He looked at her threateningly, she thought, when their eyes met. "Fuck outta' here." She whispered to herself. "Somebody died, mother fucker, and Ima be sure everybody knows I wasn't a part of that shit. Not only that, Sonny was my G, a friend and my Pato." Pato was a term of endearment between them. It is how they greeted each other.

Germaine and Sonny met in one of the many foster homes that they both had the unfortunate experience of being assigned to. She was so scared back then, Germaine remembered of Sonny. "You've seen some shit that you need to forget." Those were her first words of wisdom to fourteen-year-old Sonny, back in the day. "We ain't supposed to remember our childhood, we're supposed to get past it or die. You nothing but a Pato but be brave, okay?"

They would go on to have many enlightening conversations over the years as friends. They distanced themselves from each other, for a short time, when Germaine failed to heed her own advice and started dabbling in drugs. It started out innocently enough, partying after work on a Friday. A couple of lines of coke to take the edge off working pay check to pay check. Trying to improve her life but the music, the clubs, and the women would take precedence. Suddenly cocaine became too expensive for someone working the night shift as building security. And because the streets of New York have a different flavor for every taste bud and a lifestyle for every wallet, Germaine began smoking crack, at $10 a hit, instead of the expense of cocaine. By the time Sonny discovered that Germaine had lost her way, she had been arrested for possession with intent to traffic. Sonny visited her friend, the person who helped her through those tough years of foster home abuse, every chance she could. Germaine was released to find she had already been scheduled for an interview by the company that placed her in Barclays Bank as a starter. She was clean, had learned her lesson, and her indebtedness to Sonny would keep her that way these many years later. She worked hard, long night hours, and earned some extra cash keeping a watchful eye on Sonny during her weekly deposits. That included this last night when her dear friend and foster home protector was thrown off the 56th floor roof. Still in disbelief, and grieving, Germaine was summoned to this questioning. "I'm too angry to cry right now. Somebody is going to pay for this shit."

Germaine was acutely aware of her place on the suspect list. She came to tell her truth and without a lawyer.

"Germaine Uldaneta?" Danny extended his hand at the end of the question. "Yeah, that's me." She answered, standing up to shake his hand. "Please have a seat. My name is Detective Dan Cordova. I'm the lead homicide investigator in the murder of Sonny Rojas. My partner tells me that you and Sonny grew up together. Do you want to tell me a little about that?"

"Ain't nothing to tell bruh. We were foster siblings. Tight through the horrors, that's all."

"What kind of horrors?" Danny asked. He was writing in his notebook as she answered. He noticed her eyes were sad.

Germaine looked at the mirror, searching for a glimpse of who was sitting in on this conversation. "It's a shit life for any child, you know? We gave each other strength. Kept an eye on each other. When she slept, I watched, and vice versa. That's all, man."

"Sounds just like prison, Germaine. I see that you have done some time for possession and intent to traf..." Germaine cut him off before he could finish. "That was over ten years ago. We here for Sonny. She loved you like a brother and she loved me like a sister. I know she helped both of us. I know your story but maybe you don't know mine. I have nothing but love for that Pato, you get me? And I don't have nothing to do with her 56-floor flight, Danny do right." Germaine sat up so she could lean forward, just inches from his face. "Now you need to stop asking me bullshit questions and let me tell you what I do know." Danny did not flinch, not even at the spit spray that wet his face. He stood up and reached for the tissue box on the far end of the table and placed it in between them. He took a small recorder, turned it on, and placed it between them too. "Speak." He said. "Tell me everything you can about the night Sonny was killed." He finally wiped his face with a tissue.

"Ima say this to whoever is going to listen. Sonny was my heart." Germaine leaned down to speak loudly into the mic.

"We received two calls for access, which is unusual, but I only took one. It was the normal weekly call. Every week she calls to ask us to let three people up. Their timing is perfect. Sonny arrived first and two men arrive afterwards. By midnight, all three people are on the roof, and by twelve-thirty, they all gone. Safe and sound gone, not thrown off the roof." She finished.

"Who called to make this arrangement, Germaine?"

"Same lady, every week, you know her. Leticia. She pays the piper so she picks the music."

Danny circled Leticia's name in his note pad, the murder book, and wrote, *arranges weekly pick up,* next to her name.

"Can you describe the men?" he asked

"Same guys, every week, for the past month. Maybe more. White guys. Italianos. They look alike. I think they're brothers. The heavier one has more gray hair. The thinner one is creepy. Both have the same blue eyes." She explained.

"Height?" he continued to take notes.

"They taller than me but shorter than you, bruh."

Danny wrote down approximately 6'1" next to the rest of Germaine's description.

"They call themselves bankers but they killers, man, except they didn't kill Sonny." She went on. "They were long gone when she got thrown. Long gone. I think it was the other two fuckers."

"What other two, Germaine?"

"The monster size guys that Johnny let up."

Danny looked at Germaine's body language. Anything that would be indicative of her trying to obscure the truth, of her lying, but she continued steadily.

"He said someone had called for a fire inspection." "At midnight? Get the fuck outta' here. I knew it was bullshit. I told him something was wrong but between you and me Detective, that boy got paid to let them up."

"Can you describe the other two, Germaine?"

"Only that they were big as fuck. I was just starting my eleven-pm shift when they hit the elevator. They filled it up with muscle. Big ass, buff guys, but I didn't see their faces. Johnny let them up."

"What about the security cameras?" Danny knew there was nothing on tape showing another two men going up or coming down.

"You need to speak with the Irish boy. He was nervous and playing with all that technology when the first cop car arrived. He's a gamer, you know. Home boy got mad skills with that shit."

"You've been very helpful Miss Uldaneta. "

Danny put down his pen and murder book on the table.

"I do have one last request. I'd like to swab your mouth for a DNA sample. We're going to compare it against DNA found on the victim's body."

Germaine slammed her hand on the metal table hard enough make Maria jump from behind the glass where she was watching.

"I didn't kill no one, especially not my Pato." And she opened her mouth for swabbing.

Danny exited interrogation room A1 at the very same time that Maria entered A6 where Johnny Irish was waiting to be questioned. She had a full page of notes after watching in on the conversation between Detective Cordova and Germaine.

"How are you Johnny." She wanted to lessen the stress. It was palpable in the room.

"I'm fine, thank you." He answered, politely and shyly.

Johnny was twenty-one years old. He is the product of a typical suburban, white, and Irish upbringing. He is adored by his mother, father, and siblings so long as he doesn't flaunt his being gay in front of the family. The truth is Johnny considers himself pansexual, when asked. He does have a history of sexual relationships with older men who have a taste for twinks. Maria knew this going into his questioning.

"Let's make this quick so you can get out of here, Johnny. Germaine tells us that you arranged access for two other men to go to the roof. Is that correct?"

"No." he said immediately "I gave access to the building for alarm and fire response inspection. They arrived just before eleven o'clock."

"At night?"

"Yes ma'am, at night."

"How many men arrived? FDNY or building management?

"Two men arrived. They were both FDNY and building management." Johnny was calm, almost rehearsed, giving each answer.

"Did you have them sign in, Johnny, because I have no record of these professionals entering the building during your shift and the management office denies your claims. They tell me nothing was scheduled. Also, what happened to the security footage?"

Johnny put his head in his hands and began to shake. "I'm not feeling so good, suddenly. Can I come back to answer your questions?

Detective Cordova entered the room quickly. "I'm sorry Johnny but Barclays management has asked us to detain you, pending their pressing charges against you. They believe you are responsible for murdering Sonny Rojas." He went on. "Now I know that Sonny could kick your ass in her sleep so chances are that you did not throw her off the roof, however, I know you're involved in some way. They're holding you responsible so as not to implicate the bank or building management. Do you understand what is going on, Johnny? Can you be more helpful?"

Johnny was shaking. He turned and faced the wall to not have to look into either of the detectives' eyes while he thought about the questions. His eyes filled with tears. "Mum will be worried." He thought to himself, followed by "Jesus help me."

"Don't you have to inform me that I have a right to an attorney now?" Johnny turned to ask desperately.

Maria stepped forward. "Yes, John James Murphy Junior, would you like an attorney?"

"Yes ma'am."

Detective Soto continued to provide Johnny with the details of the Miranda warning before leading him to processing. He would be kept in a cell on premise so that they could continue questioning him with a defense attorney present.

"Can we compare notes over a sandwich, Soto?"

"Yeah, let me collect everything from CSU so far, and meet you back at our desk. I'll roll the whiteboard in."

John Murphy was fingerprinted as part of the investigation into the murder of Sonny Rojas. Although detained, the Barclays Bank and building management legal team had not yet officially filed charges. Complicity in a crime is not an easy accusation to make, at least not in the eyes of the court. Detectives Cordova and Soto knew that they would have to follow through with jailing Johnny Irish to flush out the true killers.

Fingerprinting someone so scared and visibly shaken took longer than expected. It gave Johnny time to think about a life behind bars and how his family would react. "Don't I get to make my one call?" he asked, to anyone within earshot. The area was bustling with police and detectives processing both criminals and evidence. An officer sat him down at a desk just inches from where his fingerprints were taken, and next to a phone. He handcuffed one of Johnny's arms to the metal chair arm.

"Dial nine before the number." He said as he placed the telephone in front of him.

A deep and male voice answered Johnny's call "I told you not to call me."

"I've been arrested." Johnny said through his crying. "They want to charge me with murder. You said you loved me."

"Don't say a damn thing. Ask for a lawyer. I do love you." The voice said, as he hung up.

Maria and Danny sifted through the mound of reports and results they now had, almost forty-eight hours after Sonny had been thrown from the top of the Barclays bank building on lower Manhattan.

They listed the details on a whiteboard.

Time of death: *1:20am to 1:30am*

Cause of death: *Cervical fracture with the spinal cord severed upon impact.* Danny winced while writing this on the board.

Motive: *Emotional*

"What makes you say that?" Maria asked

"A true planned execution style murder would have been quick with very little evidence. This was angry and emotional." Danny felt like Sonny was leading this investigation. "The Italianos could have done it themselves, if it was a mafia hit." "No, this was closer to home." Danny concluded.

"This is interesting." He said out loud as he read about findings on the roof. "They found rubber all over that roof that is not consistent with the roof material itself. Boot rubber and titanium shavings."

"Steel toe work boots? Johnny or Germaine?" Maria asked.

"Find out what they wear on their feet as part of their uniform"

"Yup, got it." She responded.

"She had no skin under her nails but plenty of fiber that matched the flag." He flipped the page. "Same fibers on her face, in her mouth, and in her nostrils."

Maria jumped up "They draped her in the flag to restrain her!" "I'll have it fully analyzed for any DNA."

"Sonny would have fought for her life like an animal. Check the flag for blood."

Danny continued to flip through the medical examiner's report. There was no evidence of rape. Toxicology was clean for any illegal substances. "They found traces of a

Parkinson's disease drug in her system." He said out loud. "Let's call Raya in about this, Maria, I didn't know she was sick."

The thought of Sonny having Parkinson's disease and being physically attacked angered Danny. He clenched his fists under the desk to hide his rage. Now more than ever, he was determined to make anyone involved, pay for his dear friend's death. This case was everything to him. Maria watched as he read the reports and seethed. His eyes became smaller like an animal about to attack. "Is this too personal for him?" she asked herself. "Danny, let's go for a drink tonight. This case is complicated. A little rum and coke does a body good." She smiled and patted him on the back. "Vamonos, Amigo, Sonny deserves a toast. Don't you think?"

Johnny was moved to the 'tombs' where he was placed among violent offenders waiting to be processed. The Tombs is the colloquial name for the Manhattan Detention Complex. It is the municipal jail in Lower Manhattan. It is ranked as the worst of the city's jails, both in overall conditions and in overcrowding. It holds an average of 2,000 inmates in spaces designed for only 925. Detective Cordova requested that Johnny be "broken" but watched.

El Burro watched Johnny from across the open space where inmates were allowed one hour of outdoor time. His name meant Donkey in Spanish, so named because of his large teeth and brute strength. Johnny cowered against the wall like all the young men new to prison. If fear could be turned into light, he would be glowing in neon green. He felt Burro staring from across the basketball court and their eyes met. Johnny noticed how massive the man looking at him was. Like a wall with an erection, he thought. Burro grabbed his crotch and smiled at Johnny, sticking his thick tongue out and over his teeth at him. Johnny quickly looked down. He heard the raucous laughter coming from where the man was standing. "Don't be shy pretty boy!" was shouted at him followed by "Burro, if you don't fuck him I will" Johnny looked up to see the 'man wall' walking towards him. He stood up as the man got closer so as not to have his face at groin height.

"What you in for playboy? Should I be afraid of you?" Burro said with a smile. "My name is Burro." He put out his hand.

"My my mmmy name is. They cccall me me Irish." Johnny stuttered, looking up at him, while his sweaty hand was devoured by El Burro's massive baseball glove of a hand. "Wow, that's wet! That's gonna come in handy, Irish. I like playboys with wet hands. Where else are you moist?" He adjusted his erection so that Johnny could see the magnitude of it. "Listen, I'll take care of you while you're here. Everybody is going to want those pretty green eyes looking up at them. You have to be careful, you know?" Burro was leaning in on Johnny, pressing himself against him. He stepped back an inch as a prison guard walked by in warning.

"Yyyesss, I I I know. Cccc Careful" Johnny's stuttering was out of control.

"Irish, my pretty playboy." He ran his fingers through Johnny's hair.

"I'm going to ask them to house you with me so I can protect you. Alright?" He moved in closer and put his hands down Johnny's pants. "Mmmm, I just want this in my mouth." He squeezed harder until Johnny screamed. "See, that's what pain feels like playboy. Don't ever make me angry. We only do pleasure around here. See you at home." He laughed hard and made his way across the basketball court to where he came from. Everyone congratulated El Burro on the other side of the basketball court as if they had just witnessed his wedding. Johnny watched as they all laughed and screamed in delight, many of them grabbing their own crotches in his direction.

Johnny slumped onto the ground, still in pain. He put his head between his legs and began to pray. "Dear God, please let me make it through tonight to call Detective Cordova tomorrow. I will tell him everything. Amen." He did not stutter while praying.

G

THE PLEASURE OF CRIME

"Aye Papi, aye give it to me, you're the best Daddy, aye right there." Leticia was staring at the ceiling and thinking of Sonny as Gino humped her like a dog. She felt nothing but shouted "You're going yo make me cum so hard." for effect and to accelerate his orgasm. She had mastered the art of seduction during her many years of turning tricks. Leticia raised her legs up high on Gino's back and thrust her hips in complete rhythm with his. Quickly, forcefully, biting his neck and flicking her tongue in his ear until he arched his back, trembled, and grunted before collapsing on top of her. Gino continued to orgasm as he lay on top of Leticia motionless and breathing heavy. "That was good wasn't it Papi?" She kissed his nose and rolled him off her. "I have a question for you." She shouted from the bathroom. "I have no answers." Gino said. "You have fucked me stupid." They laughed together. Leticia had turned the shower on and put her hair up. She peeked through the door. "No seriously Gino, I need you to tell me the truth."

He lifted his head up. "The truth about what? We lie about everything. We're friggin criminals Letty. What do you want the truth about?"

She emerged from the bathroom, completely naked, and stood in front of him and in all her glory. "Did you kill Sonny? You or your creepy brother? Did you arrange it?"

Gino stood up in front of her. He wiped his penis off with Leticia's 1000 thread count Egyptian cotton sheets, backed with silk jacquard, and began to get dressed. "I didn't kill the dyke and I don't know who did. You can't get emotional about this one Letty. You'll make mistakes if you do. I get it, she was good and loyal. I never had any problems with the kid but I'm telling you that we didn't do it. It wasn't even on our radar." He grabbed her chin and kissed her lips tenderly. "Now I have to go but I'm taking the smell of you with me."

"I'm still stuck on you lying about everything." She said, followed by the beautiful raspy laugh of hers.

Gino let himself out as Leticia climbed into the shower. She let the warm water run over her eyes and face as she began to sob, once again, for Sonny. "I'm so sorry." She whispered to herself.

Danny had fallen asleep at his desk at home with the murder book and all the case files underneath him. He felt Tony kiss him on the cheek. "A new lover!" he said pointing to Johnny Irish's mug shot. "He is cute."

Danny stretched, stood up, and hugged Tony tighter than he had ever before. "He may be a murderer, so cute and dangerous." "What day is it?" he continued. "I've missed you so much, Antonio." Danny loved using Tony's full given name. "Your mother knew you would be gorgeous when she named you." He would often say.

"I don't even know, hon. My entire shift was in the street. New York is burning. "He undressed and threw his clothes in a pile on the closet floor. "I need a shower and my bed."

Danny followed behind him picking up after him and filling the hamper. "Dinner?" he shouted into the bathroom.

"No, I'm good, Randy has become a barbeque master. We all had bourbon soaked ribs while on the truck running from fire to fire. It added a smoky flavor. "He was talking and laughing in the shower. "Don't get excited though, Randy had a little accident today."

"You're kidding me! What kind of accident? Is he going to be okay?" Danny yelled back into the bathroom. He knew all of Tony's fellow firemen and station mates. It made him uncomfortable in the beginning of their relationship. How could he not be concerned about these beautiful men spending so much time together and taking care of each other's every need? Tony assured him that most of the men were straight and that he was not interested in those that were not. "Love me and trust me." he would always say. "Randy is my best friend on the job."

Danny had learned to trust as much as a detective could, sparingly and carefully.

"Not sure babe." Tony went on. "A hose handle snapped back and took his thumb off. Sixteen hundred pounds of pressure per square inch just ripped it right off." He turned off the water and stepped out of the shower to find Tony standing in front of him. Tony noticed a worried look on his face. Danny was holding his boots in his hands. "These are steel toe boots aren't they." He asked nervously. "They are, why, do they turn you on?" He stepped closer to rub his naked wet body against his husband. Dan jumped back "Yes, they do. I mean no. Never mind." He fumbled and dropped the boots on the bathroom tile floor. A powdery black substance came from the boots as they hit the ground. Danny quickly scooped it into his hand. "You are such a mess maker. I'll say it again, we need cleaning help." He left Tony still drying off and primping in the bathroom to put what he had just scooped up into a sandwich bag. He shoved it into his pocket just as Tony came up behind him and kissed the back of his neck. Dan turned around to face him. "Twenty-four hours of fires and Randy losing a digit.

You must be exhausted." They kissed quickly and awkwardly. "I'm hoping that you can help me relax." Tony said. He held his semi erect member in his hand. Dan looked at him lovingly. He contemplated going down on Tony as they stood there. "God please no." he said under his breath. "You don't have to." Tony replied. "I just thought…hey are you alright." He held Danny's face in his hand. "Yes, I'm fine. It's my case. You know how much I love Sonny. And I'm sure this kid is the killer. I'm meeting with Soto."

"What?" "I thought we would have some time together. When will you be home?" Tony was serving himself a glass of red wine, still naked.

"I'll be back as soon as I can." Dan grabbed his files and murder book in one big pile and walked to the door.

"Tony, I love you." He said before leaving. He heard Tony reply as he shut the door. "I love you more." He said.

Dan sat in his car trying to catch his breath before calling Maria. She was sleeping. They had agreed to rest, overnight, before getting back to the investigation in the morning. "Why are you calling, Danny?" She heard the sobbing. "What's wrong?" His response was muffled, as he spoke with his head and phone in his hands while crying, but she heard him loud and clear. "I think Tony killed Sonny. I'm on my way."

Leticia stood on the stairs going down to her basement overlooking the operations underway with pride. She had invested in high tech, restaurant worthy equipment, to create a multi kitchen crack cocaine making facility in suburbia. Multiple pots of cocaine and baking soda were boiling on the many cook tops. All of it was powered by the solar farm she had built on her property. One hundred and twenty-three panels in total with all the power being stored in batteries bunkered underground. Every person working in her basement wore masks with industrial grade filters and lycra cover ups. No pockets to take home a gift to someone and every or any bulge could be seen. Much of what she was admiring was Sonny's idea. "We have to work smarter not harder." She said. The total investment, 98.9% pure cocaine included, was almost a million dollars. And now it was a money-making machine averaging $200,000 a day, after distribution and security fees. Leticia had already experienced her return on investment. Although the Italianos, her mafia compatriots, preached about keeping drugs out of their portfolio, they loved her setup. Their cut was for protection. They kept both the competition and cops at bay. Today would have been the day that Leticia would share the numbers with Sonny, the details of what began as her vision, and they would have celebrated with a champagne toast. She raised her glass to no one, standing on the stairs "You were my genius, Sonny Rojas. My beautiful, conniving, sweet genius! Cheers to your rise and your fall." The diabolical and incessant laughter that followed this toast was felt by everyone working in her basement. A cold chill draped over them as if a ghost had entered the space.

Detective Maria Soto looked at the black powdery substance that her partner had collected with a magnifying glass. "I can't be sure, Danny. We need to have CSI test it."

Danny was pacing back and forth while thinking out loud. "He said Randy's thumb was taken off in a hose accident! What a ridiculous lie! We need to bring Randy in for questioning without letting on to our suspicions. Fuck Maria! How do we do that? I can't go back home to him. I just can't" He began to sob again. "Why? Maybe I do need off the case now." He turned towards Maria. "What do we do?"

She had sat at her desk to write it all down as he spoke. "We need to list it all again.

1. Tony's boots may have the same roof substance we suspect the killers kicked up during the scuffle.

2. Firefighter boots are steel toe footwear which explains the titanium filings found on the roof.

3. Randy, a firefighter, had his thumb dismembered in an accident and we found a thumb at the crime scene.

4. Johnny Irish let FDNY in the building for an inspection. Two large men. Tony and Randy fit the build and description.

"Here's the question." Maria says, mid writing her list. "What is the motive?" She continued while Dan was composing himself. "We need to question Johnny Irish again but we need sleep." She stood up, grabbed some blankets and sheets out of her bathroom, and proceeded to make the couch comfortable for Danny. "We sleep tonight and head to the tombs tomorrow to question Irish. We need to link them together and it doesn't make sense to me."

"What is the difference between coincidence and actuality, Maria?" Danny questioned. He was staring into space while removing his shoes. "I don't know what?"

"Nobody lies to cover up a coincidence." Danny answered. "If we prove any connection, with either the powder or the thumb, then I know without doubt that they killed Sonny."

"The question is still why, Cordova. We must be able to arrest and keep them in prison. You know and I know that means that we must have a motive. How did the killers benefit from her death? We know it was premeditated, so what did they gain. Does Tony have any money hidden in the house somewhere? Did she have anything of his. Maybe Raya will let us have a better look around the house. We can add that visit to our list of to do, tomorrow, but for now I need to sleep brother and so do you."

Maria finished making Danny's bed on the couch. She turned around and hugged him, shocking him back to reality, from his sickened and deep thinking. "I am sorry this is happening, Danny, but it is time to be a detective and nothing more. For Sonny." She held his shoulders and looked deeply into his eyes when she said his best friends name.

"For Sonny." He repeated, several times before falling asleep and in his sleep.

THUMP

"I leave this dimension the same way I arrived, with no biologically connected human beings interested in my life or my demise. Horrible last thoughts, I know. These are the facts of my existence. I never wallowed in this truth. Instead, it motivated me to live well and to appreciate life. I don't blame my life as a G on my parent's failures or addictions. The foster system and courts turned me into a gangster. Girls and women fight daily against abuse, violence, and rape. My parents were neglectful junkies but they did not turn me into the G that I became, dysfunctional social services did. They should have helped, instead, to get my Mother and Father clean and to keep us together as a family. Sometimes I can remember my brother but I was too young and his name, as hard as I try to think back, still escapes me. I have dreamt of his face many times. More so when I was a kid feeling scared and alone. He was handsome. I used to fantasize that he was adopted by super heroes and that he would save me from the many foster parents who slapped me around just because they could. That he would fly in with a red cape filling the room just as my most hated foster father was dry humping me while his wife was in another room. Instead it was always Germaine who was my super heroine. She saved my ass so often and she was just a child herself. Germaine was hard on me to toughen me up too. I called her my survival coach. She called me Pato, lovingly. I know that she would stopped my murder had she known what was going down, specifically me.

A tiny laugh escaped from in between Sonny's lips. She felt the spray of her saliva.

So here I am falling towards seeing my parents. I have resigned myself to this trip home for a family visit. Will there be dinner and the fanfare of a family reunion awaiting me in this alternate dimension? Is my older brother already there with them? Did I have other siblings that did not survive the cruel life of addiction on the streets of New York? Is the entire family dead once I hit the ground? I really hope that there is one of us still left on this planet to write a fucking book about us.

The wind wrapped itself around Sonny's body defying gravity and lifting her back up three or four stories. She gasped as it filled her lungs with more air than they could accommodate. She wanted to cough, to expel and relieve the pressure, but could not. She flailed and panicked as she was losing consciousness. Sonny's eyes rolled back in her head and eventually closed. With her mind now off, unthinking, not speaking or remembering, her body went completely limp. She was no longer grabbing for the breeze or wind tunnel that kept her afloat. Sonny finally hit the ground.

Her neck was fractured upon impact severing her spinal cord.

I can see the cars parked near where I have fallen but I cannot feel my body. I can hear the gurgling. I feel nothing but I know I have a few minutes of thought. This is what the thump is like. Wow, it is quiet and serene. There is a man crying, screaming, and dancing around me like he has never seen a body hit the pavement. Calm down, I am dying here mister! Someone is shining a bright light in my eyes. Wait, no, I am traveling in a beam of light. They are standing in front of me. My parents are beautiful. I am with them now and the love I feel is overwhelming. I'm no longer scared, angry, or sad. I'm a G in heaven bitches! I must have done something right!

G

THE FUN IN FUNERAL

Paul Samarco sat in the back of the viewing room. He felt pinned to the wall. "Why am I here?" he thought to himself but unable to move. He planned to attend the second he watched her take her last breath. Paul and Sonny had locked eyes just before hers went matte, like that one fish eye staring at the ceiling while it lay on ice in the market. In that moment, he felt an unexplainable connection.

The story had made all the headlines in New York. He now knew her name and they had also printed the arrangement details. Paul made note of attending the service at Ortiz Funeral Home.

Now he found himself in this room, where sunlight was strangely created by lights behind stained glass depictions of bible stories. Paul couldn't make his way to the casket itself nor could he look at the picture of this young woman, placed next to it. Both reminded him that parts of her beauty, her flesh, had to be washed off his car. The sound of the body hitting the ground filled his ears as he remembered her there, next to where he slept off too much drinking, inside his vehicle. It was the same vehicle that his wife would use to take their children to school. Sonny will be with them until he can afford a new car, he thought.

He was still alone in the funeral home space with Sonny Rojas, as the newspaper and prayer cards identified her. The New York Post was turning her death into a series of articles surrounding lesbian gangsters, drug dealing, and the Italian mafia. The police chief had vowed to a deep investigation with a promise to clean it up. "Clean what up?" Paul said out loud. "They didn't even clean up your blood. Pieces of shit!" he continued, officially a grieving stranger. He stood up and walked towards the coffin looking at the picture of her next to it before turning his eyes to her body inside the box. She was dressed in a bright red top that accentuated her gray pallor. Half of the casket cover was closed, hiding whatever was mangled from the waist down. A white blanket, embroidered with crosses, was placed over her stomach and into her hands. The body was made to hold the blanket as if she was embarrassed to expose her broken self. Rosary beads were draped over the hands holding onto the blanket. The pillow under her head engulfed both sides of her face giving the impression that it was fluffier and thicker than it was. The mortician had done an amazing job of covering up all the places where Sonny's body had been battered and mangled by the fall. Paul thought back to the beautiful green sparkle of her eyes. He saw both fear and relief in them, seconds before life left her face. She grimaced upon impact leaving what looked like a deep dimpled smile as she passed. This carefully prepared body did not reflect any of that natural shine or beauty. Instead, Paul somehow knew she would be uncomfortable with the lipstick and make up that they had slathered on her. "I was there." He said to her, or rather to her corpse. "I hope you saw someone genuinely worried for you when our eyes met. Everyone should leave this planet knowing that someone cared."

"Who are you?" a female voice appeared behind him. Paul had been kneeling by the casket on the bench provided. He jumped back awkwardly, falling against Raya, as she stood there wondering who he was. "I'm sorry. Oh wow, I'm so clumsy.   I'm nobody. I mean, no one important." He was embarrassed by how his attendance would be perceived. He pulled on his blazer, straightening himself out, before extending his hand. "I am Paul Samarco. She fell next to my car. I was with her before she passed." Raya took his hand into both of hers. Tears rolled down her cheeks as she stepped towards the chairs, needing to sit, as she grasped the connection. They held hands and sat down together in unison. "Oh my, thank you, Paul." She didn't know what to say but he saw the love in her eyes. "You don't have to thank me. I don't know why I'm here, to be honest. Somehow, I feel like she invited me though." He continued "I don't think there was any pain. She looked in my eyes and smiled before she left this world." Paul did not know who this woman was but he instinctively knew to lie a little bit.

"She had beautiful green eyes." He finished, to confirm his story. Raya was now sobbing. He put his arms around her and held her to his chest. Two strangers, each grieving on opposite ends of the spectrum known as Sonny, and finding solace in each other for a moment.

Xavier walked into the viewing room with Bullet on a leash. "Raya?" He did not recognize the man holding her but could tell it was a moment of true condolence. "Is Bullet allowed in here?" he continued with his question.

"Yes. Please." Raya pulled away from the last person to see Sonny with the kindness and gentility that he deserved.

Bullet pulled the leash out of his hand, suddenly escaping the tether, and made his way towards Raya's voice and the front row where she sat. He smelled Paul, quickly in passing, but immediately turned to face the casket. It was too high for him to climb into and he began to whimper, standing and scratching at the sides. Bullet could smell his Sonny. He smelled death too. He circled her, searching for a way to reach her. Raya picked him up and let him smell her. Bullet became too frantic to hold. Paul and Xavier watched as Raya struggled to keep him from jumping in the coffin with Sonny's body. When she was finally able to put him down, without dropping him, he collapsed at her feet and howled. He did not sound like a wolf nor was it a sound that he had ever made before. It was a heartfelt acknowledgement of her death and his unconditional love. Bullet howled, or rather sobbed in pain, like a child who had just lost a parent. And the three humans in the room could not help but sob with him.

Leticia strutted into the viewing room like she was walking the red carpet at some award show. Her black hat, veil, and dress was reminiscent of Jackie Onassis and a presidential funeral. It was never her intention to be disrespectful when making these grand entrances but rather her compensation for her own emotions. The emotions she did not feel comfortable experiencing. In this case, she was grieving for someone she loved, and really cared about. She stopped in the aisle created by the chair arrangement to listen to Bullet howl. As if timed by a classic film director, Leticia perfectly orchestrated a wail, hand to her forehead, and fainted into Detective Dan Cordova's arms as he walked in behind her. He gently placed her into the closest chair available.

She opened her eyes to find Xavier fanning her with her own hat. "Welcome back." He said. He held out a plastic cup filled with water and smiled. She sipped the water and looked around to see Dan, Maria, Raya and people that she did not recognize. Bullet laid in front of the casket. He was now quiet but visibly sad. Leticia felt confused and disoriented. She looked back at Xavier, from only 6 inches away, closely. "You must be Sonny's brother. I see the resemblance. Oh my God, Papi, she looked for you for so long."

"No." Xavier answered uncomfortably. "I'm a friend of the family. Really, just a friend of Raya."

"Bullshit honey! Or maybe you don't even know you're related." Leticia laughed, that gravel laced sinister laugh, and placed the hat back on her head. She stood up to compose herself and regain her presence.

Dan stepped through the chairs, having heard her speak to Xavier. He was darker than Sonny, taller and thin, but he had an uncanny resemblance to the deceased. "Do you see it Detective? It looks like Raya found herself another Sonny."

Leticia walked towards Raya who was now seething. It was not the first time in her relationship with Sonny that Leticia said or did something that Raya felt was disrespectful to them as a couple. It happened often and Sonny was always the voice of reason and calm. "Don't let her rattle your cage." Sonny would advise. "If she finds your weakness, she will stick her finger in that wound every time you let her." Somehow Leticia understood Raya's much kept secret. Would she, could she, continue in this relationship. One where you are more alone than with the love of your life. "I never have to think about that again." She said under her breath. "They took you from me." That sentence came out louder than Raya wanted it to. Everyone turned towards her just as she finished the sentence. Raya swallowed loudly before turning towards Leticia.

"If you can't respect me here today, Letty, you should leave. Sonny lost her life working for you and the least you can do is act decently at her funeral. You come all up in here with your dramatic fainting spell and insults." Raya was losing her composure and began to yell. "LOOK IN THAT COFFIN! THAT IS WHAT IS LEFT OF

SOMEONE I LOVED." Raya was now sobbing and crying hard. "SOMEONE I ADORE! I don't even know if you had her killed? That's what you do when you feel unloved right? You hurt or kill the people you wanted to love you. SHE LOVED ME, BITCH!" Leticia was visibly shaken but stood tall and confident in front of Raya. She did not turn to look at the body. Her raspy voice betrayed her composure. "I adored her too, Raya." She put her head down. Something that Leticia rarely did. A tear rolled down her cheek as she began to leave. "And I know that she loved me too. Deal with it!"

Leticia left quietly. Bullet never moved, even while Raya was screaming at the top of her lungs. Tony and Germaine came in, separately, to find the atypical somber of a funeral. Dan leaned in towards Maria. He whispered, "Collect DNA from everyone that you can here." She nodded yes. He stood up to deliver Sonny's eulogy as Raya had requested of him.

"Don't cry" He heard Sonny's voice as he stood behind the podium. A picture of Sonny smiling with Bullet on her lap was projected on the screen behind him as he began:

"Sonny Rojas was born a good person. We all are but some of us are forced to overcome challenges from the moment we are born. She shared her life stories with me at a time that I needed to hear a successful survival story.   She nurtured me back to good health both physically and mentally. Her friendship was unconditional and she was loyal. Sonny loathed her life as a criminal. Outside of this gangster façade she wanted a decent life with her love, Raya. I remember talking to her about her wedding and her eyes would light up, along with that killer dimpled smile. Even on the streets she was known as a G with compassion. Her death was senseless and irrational but emotionally charged. I know this because everyone we have interviewed or interrogated has said the same thing; Sonny would never cross anyone. She was full of love and she was smart. Today we say goodbye to my beautiful friend. The person who cared enough about me to save my life and set me on the straight and narrow. That's who she was. Selfless. Exit strategy! She said those words to me often. This was a complete blindside." The detective's voice began to quiver. "We will not rest until we find the person or people responsible for her death. That is my commitment to her. I will miss you, G." He could no longer hold back the tears. Everyone was moved to tears at that point. Detective Soto offered everyone tissues and water, in hard plastic cups, which she kept track of and labeled at the end of the service. She collected, hopefully, a DNA sample from everyone in attendance.

Leticia stood behind the viewing room door where no one could see her. It was gapped enough for her to watch and listen to Dan deliver the eulogy. Her silk handkerchief was soaked with her tears. She dabbed carefully so as not to ruin her makeup. "I will miss you too." She said to herself, as she continued to watch through the gap.

Raya hugged every person who attended and thanked them for coming. The embrace with Xavier was warmer and lasted longer, Leticia noticed. "Hmm, bodies touched with that hug, and Sonny isn't even buried yet. Puta!" She was analyzing it all from afar. They were heading out, towards her, so she turned to leave before they found her still there, watching and crying.

"You can throw me out but you can't stop me from finding out who your new boyfriend is." She said out loud and in the parking lot of Ortiz Funeral Home. She looked up at the beautiful blue sky, into the sun, and put her Hermes sunglasses on. "Right Sonny?"

G

G

PATO

Germaine made it back to her apartment after the funeral, without stopping. It was a true testament of her inner strength. Every cell in her body tried to steer her towards a bar, where she could get crazy drunk, but she had to work tonight. Funeral dramatics are always fun but this was above normal and made for television or film, she thought to herself.

It was still daytime, just before sunset, and the sky was glowing an exceptionally deep orange. She opened all the window coverings to let the last of this beautiful light in. It was her ritual, when the sun was shining, to let it fill her humble abode as much as possible. Vitamin D deficiency was a common downfall of those who work the midnight to morning shift and Germaine suffered from S.A.D. Seasonal affected disorder was not something to play with. It was a form of depression that she was acutely aware could lead her back to the bad habits that ruined her life, for a while.

The difference today would be that she would have to conquer her demons without her unofficial sponsor, Sonny. She shuddered at the thought.

The light blinded her as she bent down to put her glass on the coffee table in front of her. Pictures of Germaine and Sonny were strewn all over the sofa. She had gone through her boxes of memories earlier in the day, before the funeral.

"I'm going to get all of the tears out of me before I go see you in a box today, Pato. You're not going to have me crying snot ugly in public." She said out loud while looking up at the ceiling, and to the Sonny ghost she imagined.

Her left hand picked up the closest picture to her in unison with her right hand picking up the glass. The taste of Jack Daniels Tennessee honey on her lips and Sonny's smile brought her right back to their youth. "I didn't think either one of us would go so early but my money was on me departing first." She spoke to the photograph. "You convinced me that we would all leave this planet, elderly, and on the up and up, Pato." Germaine's nickname for Sonny went hand in hand with the taste of Jack. "What happened?" She leaned back on the sofa, closed her eyes, and wiped away that one tear drop that she could not contain.

"Wake the fuck up. You shouldn't be drinking by yourself." Germaine sat up, shocked at the clarity of Sonny's voice. "I'm not here, but I'm here, you know." Sonny was sitting on the coffee table in front of her. "Don't have a heart attack now." The apparition said.

"What the fuck?" Germaine stood up and ran to the bathroom to run some cold water on her face and the back of her neck. A voice from the living room said "You can't wash me away. And I don't know how much speaking time I have. Come back here."

She knew deep down inside that this was her grief manifesting hallucinations. Germaine had not slept well since she found out about Sonny being murdered. It wasn't that she had died that hurt her but that someone had taken her life so viciously. It was the gruesome murder, and that Sonny fell 56 floors to her death, that consumed Germaine's sleep. Combine this anguish with the normal grief and now, Jack Daniels Tennessee Honey, and "it's no wonder I hear her voice." That she could see Sonny sitting on the coffee table was another kind of crazy altogether! "Do I talk back to it?" She asked to herself.

"I'm not an it, mother fucker, it's me. I need you to talk to me."

Germaine looked down to see the glass on the table was empty. She had fallen asleep on the sofa and many of the pictures were scattered on the floor. Incredibly, she was staring at her own body, in a fetal position, sleeping and snoring. This was an out of body experience with Pato the friendly ghost! "I hear you. I'm not sure what is happening." Germaine hesitated to converse with Sonny. "Please, let this be the one and only time, Sonny. I can't do cray cray comfortably." She said.

Sonny stood up and leaned in close to the body sleeping on the couch. "Wow, you still snore like a Mack truck." The ghost laughed.

Germaine gave the whole scenario a few seconds of thought. This is nothing more than a dream, really, because I'm watching myself sleep. I'll just go with it and see where it leads. Mental note; no more Jack D., or drinking, for me. If nothing else, this apparition would insure her sobriety. "Another part of my life to thank you for, Sonny." She said this barely under her breath but the dead Sonny standing in the room and speaking to her, heard it.

"That's great news. I love you my G. I will always be with you. Friends forever! Never forget that." Sonny said. "Now before I lose you, I need you to think back. Who entered the elevator at Barclays Bank? Look in to your memories. You didn't pay attention but it is there."

Germaine let herself drift back. Suddenly, she was once again, part of her own body, sleeping curled up and uncomfortable on the small sofa. She wanted to argue with Sonny that she did not see their faces, only their bodies, but everything began to move before she could counter.

In slow motion, she found herself walking to the starter desk for her shift. She looked around. Irish looks nervous, uncomfortable, and her eyes slip down to his keyboard. Delete! He has hit the delete key. She never noticed that before. His voice echoes in this surreal dimension of going back to the past. "Fire inspection started early." He says. There aren't any names in the log? Germaine had questioned him. "It all goes to HQ from now on, online." He explains.

Why would I not confirm that? Germaine thinks to herself, even in this suspended state. Slowly, her head turns around to see two men just entering the service elevator. I still can't see the faces. Johnny Irish is nervously chattering behind her. At the time, his conversation required acknowledgement, and that Germaine would stop looking at the elevator, and instead stop to answer him. She doesn't have to answer now. Suspended in time and speaking with a ghost, Germaine is concentrating on every detail of these men that she can see. Typical firemen, they are big men: they appear Caucasian, thick necks, wearing the standard FDNY clothing and gear. "What am I looking for?" she says before she spots it. THE RING! One of them is wearing a unique black titanium wedding ring on his left hand. The front of the ring is flat and squared off. Two sets of initials are engraved on the flat part of the ring, with a large bright shiny round diamond in between the initials. "I don't know how I missed it then but I could not stop looking at it during Sonny's funeral, even with all of the drama. The initials are AC DC. The fireman is Tony Cobian!

Germaine gasped for air and awoke in time to get ready for her security night shift. It all felt real enough to her to trigger a search for Detective Maria Soto's business card, tossed in her kitchen junk drawer, after her semi-arrest and questioning. She dialed the number but hung up the phone quickly. "How do I explain this shit?" she considered, before redialing.

"Detective Soto. Hello, how may I help you."

"Yeah, it's me Germaine Uldaneta. I don't know if you remem..."

She was quickly cut off by the voice on the other end. "Of course, I remember you, Germaine. What can I do for you?"

"I had a fucking weird dream last night. Sonny came me. She was in my crib and talking to me. I'm not crazy or high. seriously. Anyway, the dream helped me to remember something."

The detective could be heard shuffling paper on her side of the call.
"I'm just going to write this down, Germaine, what did you remember?"

"I remembered something about one of the firemen who went upstairs in the elevator. I couldn't see his face, but I could see his left hand and arm. He was wearing a unique ring. like a wedding band."
"Go on." Maria was writing as Germaine spoke.
"It is black, with a diamond in the center, in the middle of initials AC DC. It's the same ring that Detective Cordova

wears and that Tony Cobian was wearing today at the funeral. "They're married, right?"

"I'm going to need you to come in and sign your testimony, Germaine. Okay?"

"Yo, I have to go to work this evening. I won't get paid and I could get fired."

"I'm sending a squad car to pick you up. We can speak to the building management. You're helping to solve a crime that happened on their property. That's the best security that they can hire. Besides that, what would Sonny do?"

"Yeah. Alright. I get it. I'll be ready when they get here."

Germaine looked across the room to the coffee table where she saw Sonny sitting there, in what she was sure was a dream. As clear as day, she heard the voice. It was combined with her own breathing sounds, in the quiet of the room.

"Thank you, G."

Germaine answered before heading into the bathroom.

"Forever, Pato."

G

G

WHY'S, LIES, AND TIES

While they would never cover up a crime, both Detectives Cordova and Soto knew that Johnny Irish had been roughed up while held in the tombs. They would never know the details but had asked for him to be properly "received" by El Burro. Irish was back in a holding cell at the NYPD Detective Bureaus Forensic Investigation Unit now, where Dan & Maria were compiling the final data.

Germaine had remembered something key to the investigation. Maria refused to give Danny any details to keep him from being emotionally affected, she said. He could only imagine since his probing, and instincts, had already implicated his very own husband at the crime scene. To what extent, was still under review.

Every person at the funeral had unknowingly submitted a DNA sample to the crime labs. DNA sampling was tedious and meticulous work where it applies to evidence in a crime. It is used to establish a link between the victim and the suspect in an investigation. The range and depth of testing points to either parental, forensic, and or genetic testing in looking for similarities. Sonny didn't have any cells underneath her fingernails, for example, that could identify a killer. She had been wrapped in the flag before being tossed off the roof of the building. Instead, Dan had asked for any DNA evidence on the flag, that matched someone at the funeral. Also, he was looking for a connection between Sonny and anyone there, that was not disclosed for whatever reason.

Leticia is a brilliant woman and while her delivery at the funeral was obnoxious and sarcastic, Danny paid attention to her identifying a resemblance between Sonny and Xavier. He never noticed it until Letty pointed it out. Raya may have had enough with Leticia's antics but she saw it too and both detectives noticed her fleeting, yet shocked, reaction. Murder book note: Question Raya about Xavier.

Dan and Maria greeted Germaine upon arrival. "Thank you for your help Miss Uldaneta. Sonny meant the world to me and I know that she did to you too." Dan offered his handshake. Germaine responded. She could see the pained love in his eyes and could only imagine the turmoil within him. Sonny told her many times "Danny is my family, G. Don't ever doubt him and don't ever fear him. He is a good cop."

"Sonny would call this un arroz con culo." She said to him

"A rice and ass situation." He translated in English. "Yes, she would, Germaine. It's a mess that doesn't make sense. And she would be right but maybe with your help we can get closer to the truth. Please have a seat." He pulled out the chair for her.

Maria pushed a microphone in front of her and pulled a yellow lined legal size pad out of the drawer to place in front of them all for her note taking. "We are going to record everything you tell us tonight, both on paper for your signature, and on tape so that we don't get anything wrong in the future. Are you alright with that, Germaine?"

"You know I am. I'm here, aren't I. Can I get a glass of water too, please?"

"Absolutely." The water was delivered to the interrogation room without any of them leaving to get it. Clearly, they were being watched and listened to.

Dan Cordova listened to Germaine repeat the details of her evening and memory of the night Sonny was killed. His own recollection was sparked by her testimony. The way Tony avoided every visit from Sonny with an emergency at the firehouse, or a change in schedule. She always seemed genuinely disappointed so what was his issue with her? Whether her murderer or an accomplice, there is always a motive that ties people to a crime. One thing that both Maria and Danny knew for sure was that Tony was not an innocent bystander.

What did not make sense was that he worked with her to save me, years ago. They worked together to bring me back to good health, and to better my life. They did so organically and without my knowledge, until I was back to normal. I assumed a relationship had developed from that collaborative experience but he was not a Sonny fan, now that I think of it.

I once pressed him. It was her birthday and in typical form, he found a reason to disappear just before she and a few friends arrived. "Is something wrong between you two? Why do you always find a reason to go, just when she is arriving. She has noticed and it hurts her feelings. She is my friend, Tony." He stayed and he looked her in the eye and said "I am a fireman. I love you and him." Gave me a kiss in front of everyone and finished with. "Happy Birthday, Sonny, but I have to go again." They hugged and all night, all who attended gushed over his sweetness, but it never felt genuine. Something was awry. We just all let it go.

Now we need to find out why.

Danny came out of his own memories to ask Germaine the final question in her interview. "Miss Uldaneta, does the ring you describe look like this one?" He held his own wedding ring right in front of her face. "Yes." She answered.

"Let the record show that the evidence, now photographed, and included in this testimony is Detective Cordova's own wedding band. He and his husband, Antonio Cobian, wear custom made matching bands. Germaine Uldaneta has identified Antonio Cobian as one of the fireman who entered the Barclays Bank building to do a routine inspection on the very same evening that Sonny Rojas was murdered. This testimony is consistent with the steel toe boot filings found on the roof that also match Antonio Cobian's standard issued FDNY boots. Miss Rojas was thrown from this roof to her death.

Germaine was catered to the dinner of her choice, via take out, while all was formally recorded. They had enough to pick Tony up and had requested a search warrant of his firehouse, in the interim.

Dan entered the interrogation room where Johnny Irish cowered in a corner, like a scared puppy. "John, John, Johnny. How are you feeling, Sir?" he asked

He placed the recorder in front of him before he could answer the question. "I'm f f fine." He stuttered nervously. Johnny searched the large one way glass behind Dan Cordova's chair for any sign of someone watching them. "There is no one on the other side, Johnny. Just you and me. You've been through a lot this week. I understand there were people who made you uncomfortable while you were in the tombs. I want to protect you but I need you to be honest with me."

"Yes." His soft voice made him appear childlike but John was very much the adult who was good at his twink persona.

Dan placed his wedding band in front of Johnny. "Do you recognize this ring? Have you seen it on anybody else, other than me?

"No. I have not."

"You have not seen this ring on my beautiful husband, Johnny?" Dan pushed

"I, I, I said no." the nervous stutter resurfaced

"Don't get nervous Johnny. Is he fucking you? I really hope it is that simple and that he has not involved you in a murder. You understand the repercussions of lying to me, here, don't you?" "I'm not asking as a scorned lover. I am the lead Detective investigating the murder of Sonny Rojas, who was thrown from the roof that you are paid to secure. It happened on your watch. You do understand?" Detective Cordova placed pictures of Sonny's twisted and bloody body on the sidewalk in front of Johnny. "I'm going to ask you again. Please think. Have you seen my husband wearing this ring?

"I have. Everyone knows you, you, you two are married." Johnny stuttered again.

"Exactly." Danny leaned in close to Johnny's face, his voice now stern and threatening. "He was wearing it the night you arranged for him to be on the roof in wait for Sonny, remember that? The real question is why would you help my husband commit a crime?"

"Do you know how many people the man you met at the tombs, El Burro, has killed in prison, while fucking them, Johnny? Danny opened the folder to read it for effect. "Nine! Nine young pretty boys, just like you. He raped and killed them all." "We should pull him out of general population, but again that depends on you tonight"

"Please. Don't leave me there. Tony didn't ask me to. He did not. Randy did"

"Randy?" Danny stood up to think. He walked around the table and stood behind Johnny now. "Randy was the second inspection officer?"

"Yes." Johnny answered

"Why would Randy be involved, John? Do you have any idea? Dan was now sitting on the table next to John.

"Yes. We are in a relationship. He said he loved me but I know I'm just a blow job, now."

"Who knows about this relationship?"

"Tony and Randy. T tony threatened to tell Randy's wife." He was crying.

Danny pushed slid his own water in front of him "Here, have a drink."

"My husband is blackmailing Randy? Do you know what that means?"

"Yes, I know what that means. And yes, he is Dan.

Detective Cordova felt emotionally drained. "Thank you, Johnny. Is there anything else I should know?"

"Yes. T t tony bit off Randy's thumb."

Maria was waiting outside of the interrogation room, behind the glass, where Dan had finished questioning Johnny Irish.

"Are you okay?" she asked.

"Run with me." He answered. Dan was rushing to include John's testimony as part of the request for a search warrant of city property, namely the firehouse where both Tony and Randy were assigned.
"Am I okay? I will be, Soto, but right now I am more determined than most to bring this case to justice."

"I know." She said, still running behind him. "I know how much Sonny meant to you and how much this is all tearing you apart. You can no longer be part of this investigation, Detective Cordova.

He stopped in his tracks to reply "I understand. And I'm just finishing my shift. This is not about Sonny anymore! I have been living with a stranger. It has all been a lie. I don't even understand why, Maria."

He took the ring out of his pocket. "If it were not that this ring is now crucial evidence to our case, I would flush it down the toilet with the rest of my life."

"I'm sorry Danny. I really am. Let's do what we do best, partner. I'm on my way to the lab. Some of the DNA results are in."
"I'll meet you there." He said.

Danny arrived at the lab to find both Maria and the technician, Farooq, excited about the findings and the case. He was able to push for the search warrant and it was being endorsed by a judge who expressed how disturbing the thought of any first responder being involved in this case. The media would take the cities commitment to clean up organized crime, because of Sonny's murder, and turn it around viciously if a city employee was involved. The case had become highly visible and on top of his life being in turmoil, Dan now had the added stress of political pressure.

"You two are beaming and I cannot be shocked any more if you tried. What did you find?"

The lab technician began "Interestingly enough, as indicated by the physical similarities noted by Detective Soto, the deceased Sonny Rojas and Xavier are indeed siblings. They share the same maternal DNA but not paternal markers."

"What do we do with that? Do either of them know? I can't tie this to a murder, Detective Soto, any ideas?" Dan responded.
"It gets a little easier to juicier." Maria said. "Give him the rest of the results, Farooq."

"Why yes. In addition, we have concluded that Sonny Rojas and Antonio Cobian both share the same maternal and paternal DNA, making them 100% siblings, Detective Cordova.

These three individuals are related. And before you ask, by conclusion and further matching, Antonio Cobian and Xavier are genetically confirmed to be half-siblings as well."

The room began to spin. Dan could not remember when he last had something to eat, at that exact moment. He felt weak, faint, and confused. "He knew she was his sister?" He said. "The fire story. There was never a grave to visit. A death date. He never cried. He told the story as if it was a defense mechanism instead of something that truly happened. I'm a fucking detective and I missed all of the indications." He stumbled and kneeled to prevent himself from falling. Dan looked up at Maria. He was tired, embarrassed, and confused. "I can't, Soto. I'm too emotionally involved. I can help you, but I don't know"

"I've got this Danny. I'm taking you to my place to sleep. There is a team heading out to search the firehouse. We cannot have his husband involved in that now. Optics, emotions, politics, any ties my friend. I am going to pick up Xavier for questioning too. If the plot, however twisted, involves him then we need to keep him away from Raya."

They gathered the murder book, all the new lab reports, and headed out to Maria's car. "Drop me off at Leticia's house, Maria."

Why?" "Are you sure?" Maria asked.

 "I'll be fine." He replied "I need to speak with her. Ask her some questions. And I need to let her enjoy my heartbreak, to get the answers."

The search warrant was executed in SWAT like fashion simply to feed the media machine that was following the case like white on rice. West 10th Street, in Manhattan, was closed off on both sides of the street to prevent any FDNY vehicles, including fire and rescue trucks, from leaving the facility. Adjacent squads picked up all of FDNY squad 18's calls during the search and seizure. It was the first of its kind in New York City and certainly a blemish on the Gay village altogether. The underlying first responder competition that has always existed between the FDNY and NYPD was in full force at the executive level but on the ground, the police felt like they were raiding their own safe spaces. While it was visibly quite the show of force it was delicately carried out too. Tony and Randy were handcuffed and paraded on camera more than normal. Firemen gone rogue was better optics than the gay mafia running amok in the city, right under law enforcements noses. Leticia had already paid a significant part of her cut to Gino, as part of the overall pay off to steer attention away from their doings. La Cosa Nostra and the gay mafia worked together like a well-oiled machine. They protected each other.

Danny awoke from a fourteen-hour sleep, more accurately described as a complete collapse, in one of Leticia's grand spare bedrooms. He was not only dodging the media but separating himself completely from the case. Detective Soto knew where to find him but no one would dare tread on Leticia's property or even suspect that he was here. It was a delicate situation whereby any of his work on the case could easily be misconstrued as obstruction. How did you not know or suspect anything, Detective? They would ask. "Not a clue of his disdain for Sonny, over the years?"

He would ask these questions himself if he were looking in from the outside. Now, his naiveté and being blinded by love, could free Sonny's killers and put them back on the street, if they were not careful.

Leticia knocked on the door. "Do I hear you stirring around for breakfast, handsome? Come honey, you need to eat, and clothing is optional at my table." He could hear her laughing all the way back to the kitchen. "Is it sick that her voice somehow feels like home?" he asked himself.

The coverage was on every news channel and CNN. Letty was watching a press conference where both the Chief of Police, and the head of the Fire Department, were answering questions and promising justice for Sonny. They also committed to "cleaning up." Media had camped themselves outside of Randy's house and a family representative had given the "we are all trying to understand what has happened and please give us the privacy to deal with it speech." You could hear some of the questions being shouted when they walked away from the microphones. "Did his wife know he was having a homosexual relationship with a 21-year-old male?" they yelled out. They knew no one would answer that question. It was an informational broadcast. Left to linger for conversation. Danny was sure they were looming around his home, or worse, around the precinct. "Homely can handle the media." Leticia said, as if she could read his thoughts, while expressing her disdain for Detective Soto.

"I dreamt about us having breakfast together." She said with a smile. "Yes. It was beautiful. I reached for your sausage." That raucous laughter and her uncomfortable jokes were just Leticia's way of coping and her attempt to take Danny's mind off everything that was brewing. He sat down to her amazing Bustelo coffee and lavish breakfast. He felt himself relaxing in her presence and suddenly he was hungrier than he had ever been. "I can't remember that last time I ate, thank you Letty."

"Aye Papo, you don't have to thank me, we have been through so much. Eat, eat, Sonny is watching us. Together as a happy family again. Just like the old days. Home fries?" she passed the plate to him. It did feel like solace. Dan ate quietly. They both did. While watching the updates. For a moment, he hid in this delusion and relaxed, knowing full well that his life was a mess outside of this hiding spot. They moved to Leticia's sun room when breakfast was over to speak. Dan was surprised at how amiable she was to speak with him about all that has transpired. Normally he would be suspicious, but he no longer trusted his detective skills.

"I have to ask you some questions Letty, in an unofficial capacity. They are for my own peace of mind. Are you alright with that?"

"I'm disturbed by you asking me for the truth with a lie, Danny."

He didn't understand. "What do you mean?"

"If any of my answers point to a crime, the questions become official. Leticia always smiled behind one of her brilliant statements. You and I both know that you are down but you are not out. You are a detective, through and through, and my favorite one on the force/"

"True, Letty. And I will forever admire your genius, even if you don't use it for good. He made her laugh loudly.

"What is good, Danny?" she smiled "Both good and bad have short shelf lives." "Some Marijuana cartels are now thriving and legitimate businesses, just a short drive from here. Yet how many of my Gs' are doing time, long sentences, for carrying a few ounces of Kush?" "I know you don't want to debate bullshit with me, Papo, ask your questions." She was refilling his coffee when he asked.

"Why did you have me beaten so severely, Leticia?"

The question rattled her. He saw the sadness on her face. Dan knew Leticia Maldonado well enough to know that anyone questioning one of her business decisions would incur her anger, not this face of regret. "I have wanted to tell you this for so long, Dan Cordova." She used his full and real name rather than any of her terms of endearment. He understood that this was an official explanation and possibly of a crime. She looked directly into his eyes. "Antonio paid me to. Not just me but the Italianos. And not just with money either. He insured his own safety and solicited the contract by holding every fire insurance contract over our heads. He had compiled an entire package for the federal RICO boys." RICO stood for Racketeer influenced and Corrupt Organizations. Alerting any federal authorities, especially about fire code infractions, could cease operations for every crime family or organization. Not to mention, federal responders would assail them with a much larger pit bull kind of investigation. "The Italianos fight that shit every day." She continued. "They didn't need more and if it happened, my life was over too." "The original contract that he requested was to kill you. He wanted to hurt Sonny by going after everything and everyone that she loved, and he wanted it to be gruesome, Papo." She visibly trembled as she raised the coffee cup to her mouth. "He is a special kind of loco, you know." "I stopped your murder. I could hear you from inside here. You are my family." She began to cry. "I ran in and stopped it. And I called Sonny to help you." Dan put the tissue box closer to her. "Go on." He said. "What is there to tell? When we spoke, after you were taken away alive, I said kill me! Enough! I told Gino and Louie, you tell your people to kill me because I was not going to let Tony tell me what to do. The Italianos turned the hit around and convinced him that it was in his better interest to carry on with whatever vendetta he had with Sonny or you, by himself. The next thing I know, you are marrying Mr. Loco, so I thought it was over. The shelf life, Danny, bad became good!" "Anymore questions before I start my day?" she stood up to walk back to the kitchen with their coffee cups.

"Yes, Letty, did you know that Tony is Sonny's brother?"

The tray she was holding dropped to the ground shattering all that was on it. "Aye Dios mio!" "He is the boy who raped her?" She put her hands to her face in horror.

Dan stood up. His chest was pounding. This was the first he had ever heard of this and didn't know how to process the information, Leticia gathered up all the pieces of china and placed them on the tray. She realized Danny didn't know. She would have to betray Sonny's confidence and tell him the story.

"Sit down Papo. I promised her that I would never tell her secrets, especially the one she covered up so well, but you need to know." They sat side by side. Danny cried for his friend, not her death, but that her childhood, as horrible as he knew it to be, had truly been incomprehensible. Leticia cupped his hand with both of hers. In this moment, she was more human than he had ever known her to be.

"Sonny told me the story of the crack houses and heroin dens that they grew up in. We all heard them over and over. Her older brother was, as she would explain, beyond evil and a seasoned criminal, even as a boy. He could kill a stray cat, comfortably, and just for the fun of it. And apparently, he was a much sought after child sex worker, thanks to their father. He sent him out to suck dick all day long, just to keep his heroin coming. One day, their father was angry because a trick had beaten and fucked her brother raw, but worse had stolen all the boy's money. He came back bleeding and broke at a time when their father needed a fix badly. Daddy wanted to send him back out and Sonny remembers her brother volunteering her, to take his place, while he healed.

Her mother was adamant, upset, and she said no. She fought with the father, and stood her ground. She did this many times for Sonny. Her mother was a crack addict but even in her high, she tried to save Sonny from that life. It was too late for the first born. When the brother came back from another trick, with his father's dope, he was crazier and eviler than ever. This thirteen-year-old boy, she told me, raped her repeatedly and viciously that night. Their mother came out of her high to catch him in the act. Sonny was 6 years old and had passed out several times from both the pain and trauma. Her mother beat the brother with whatever she had to get him off Sonny's limp and bloody body and when their father came to, amid the commotion, he took over and threw him out of the abandoned building that they lived in.

Tony came back before sunrise and in his rage, he set the building on fire, while everyone slept. Their father died in that fire. The boy was adopted after doing time in juvenile detention. Because of the circumstances, his parents being homeless and addicts, the court granted him leniency. Sonny remembered it all in pieces, thanks to therapy, and what she remembered she also covered up. She searched for her brother just to understand and have closure." Leticia took a deep breath and looked into Dan's eyes. "I didn't know Tony was that brother, Papo, but now it all makes sense. He still had a lot of pain and revenge left in him."

"And Xavier, Letty, did you know about a younger brother?"

"Yes, her mother was raped in one of the shelters. She again saved Sonny's life giving herself to the rapist, that went after her daughter, and so that Sonny could live a better life in foster care. In one of the parental visits, her mother was noticeably pregnant. She found out that she had a younger brother, as an adult, and was always searching for him. She wanted to give him a good life, she always said, the love and comfort that she always wanted"

"I don't think Raya knows who he is, although I believe you raised her suspicion, Letty." Danny thought out loud.

"I thought about that shit." She was regaining her tough composure. "I think Raya is Sonny's gift to Xavier and vice versa. I had him checked out and followed. Don't judge me." That notorious laugh again. "At first I thought he knew and maybe the older brother used him as bait, but no honey, he is clueless and squeaky clean. He is an artist and too mushy a man for me, but he is in love with her."

"I don't think I'll disrupt that apple cart." Danny smiled down at Leticia and leaned in to hug her hard. "I'm sorry that I caused you any pain Papo." She said into his neck, during the hug.

"And I need to tell you that you are my family, Leticia Maldonado, I forgive you and I love you." He said.

Leticia had not heard those words since her mother hugged her as a little boy. This time she was loved for who she really was, not just authentically, but with all her flaws. She was overwhelmed with emotion and sobbed heavily into Dan Cordova's shoulder before pulling away and making a joke, in her usual way. There was always something to laugh about, Leticia thought. "Is there any fucking involved with this I love you?" she asked

"No. I forgave you for fucking me already." He winked at her

'

They both laughed.

"A girl has to try." She smiled.

"Danny called Detective Maria Soto to inform her of his conversation with Leticia Maldonado. They now had a motive, locked tight. Letty agreed to provide an affidavit, if she did not have to appear in court. The Italianos secured that agreement for her. She was right, there is never an unofficial conversation with a law enforcement officer.

Antonio Cobian and Randy Lang are incarcerated awaiting sentencing. They both face life in prison with no possibility of parole. Johnny Irish was sentenced to 20 years for aiding and abetting a premeditated murder. He was killed in jail less than a month into his term. Antonio Cobian was charged with that murder and it was added to his file and sentence.

Dan has deep and brilliant conversations with Ms. Maldonado every chance he can. She is the smartest and most beautiful woman he knows. He tells her this often, along with "I like men, and we will never fuck, but you are my family."

Detective Soto agreed to lose the DNA report connecting Sonny and Xavier. The relationship between Raya and Xavier was not only healthy but her chance at happiness. It is what Sonny wanted. They went on to discover that Sonny had aligned these stars for Raya. She knew her Parkinson's Disease would progress and prepared her exit strategy carefully. It was selflessly designed for both of them.

Danny assured that all evidence of her plan was a secret well protected. As far as he was concerned it was the single most incredible act of love that he had ever witnessed.

G IS FOR GOODBYE

Xavier packed the car with the few items that Raya was taking. "I have never seen a woman pack so little." He said to her smiling. "Are you complaining?" Raya asked. "No, not at all, I didn't realize I was going to share the rest of my life with a super hero." He kissed her gently on the forehead. Raya leaned in for a full hug. They were constantly together and it felt so good. Watching the news, going back to all the pain and horror, it was a wonder that they had survived it all. She could feel Sonny with them sometimes. Xavier mentioned it before she dared to, for fear of appearing crazy. "I feel protected by her, for some reason. I think we all are." He shared. Raya felt the same way. And Bullet often sat or laid down as if someone was petting him. Raya abided by Sonny's very detailed steps to love and freedom without her, to the tee. She had sold and gifted most of their possessions together. She adhered to the money details, the travel itinerary, and of course had fully embraced spending her life with Xavier. He was not her, she often reminded herself. Xavier is a free spirit while Sonny was all encompassing and a protector. She has left that behind, in a sense, by taking care of all their needs. And hey, Raya thought, if it doesn't work out for whatever reason, she would still take care of him like Sonny asked.

Xavier and Bullet had also bonded. He was easy to love.

Danny stopped by to say his goodbyes. He was more comfortable with himself than he had ever been before. She mentioned this to him and he said, "Sonny left us all with some wonderful gifts." I know that I can count on him should I ever need anything. Ours is an unbreakable bond.

 Even Leticia Maldonado showed signs of being human. Raya had heard that her testimony was critical to the case that locked Sonny's killers up forever. It was afterwards that Leticia sent flowers and an apology. It read "She loved you more than anything in the world. Don't ever forget that." Technically, the words "I'm sorry." did not appear on the card but Raya knew they were intended. And Dan confirmed that she was never the enemy but simply in charge of her world. That world of gangsters, where love is often absent, but always sought after.

Paul Samarco stayed in touch and they had exchanged letters since her relocation. There was a connection between them since he was the last person to see life in Sonny's eyes. It was almost as if some of her love for life had transferred to him in the instant in which they had looked into each other's eyes. He would never forget, he said, her beautiful gaze. It was as if she was consoling him. He walked away from that traumatic experience a more compassionate and empathetic man. Raya knew they would be friends forever.

Zamora, Spain, had become home for Raya and Xavier. The lake known as Sanabria is one of the biggest in the area and in Spain. It measures 1.5 kilometers wide, 3 kilometers long and has a depth of around 50 meters. The many different types of water activities are carried out on the lake, and in summer, the area is filled with hundreds of people enjoying themselves by and on the water. This was their new haven. Away from the hustle and bustle of New York but most importantly, it took them far away from where Sonny's life was ended.   Raya found comfort in keeping with Sonny's wishes. It was the perfect place to start anew. Xavier and Bullet took to the country, the language, and the serenity as if they belonged here all along. The size of Sanabria lake allowed them to explore a new "spot" every day, so far.   Many creatives called this part of the world home. Raya studied the people, the culture, and the language with the hopes of eventually finding work here. She also allowed herself this time to mourn, and properly grieve, her great love. Xavier understood and encouraged her respite.

Bullet laid down at Xavier's feet watching the small boats swaying on the water. They were tethered and often bounced causing a sound below the hull that sounded very much like a dog's bark. His ears perked up, each time, yet he had learned the difference in sounds now and simply enjoyed being with his human Daddy. Xavier painted, or wrote poetry, inspired by the people, colors, and passion of Spain. Raya watched them both, falling in love with them repeatedly, each time she did. She had fully immersed herself in this new home and was listening to her Spanish language lesson tapes while Xavier did his thing.

"Gracias, Sonny." She said while listening. "Muchisimas gracias"

Sonny 's spirit washed over them all like a cleansing. This street thug, once feared by some and looked down upon by others, had become the angel she was always meant to be. Every horrible childhood experience and her willingness to not just survive them all, but to thrive while forgiving, was a universal plan. She would not be remembered as a G, but instead as someone who epitomized love. And that is truly gangster.

THE END

Stay Gangsta'

ABOUT THE AUTHOR

Joie Lamar published her first novel, volume 1 of a 2-part memoir called Mambo Lips in 2016. The much-anticipated second part, Salsa Hips, hit book store shelves shortly after. They both sold quickly; over 100k copies all over the world. More impressive than this feat, for a new writer with LGBTQ content, was that Mambo Lips became part of the curriculum and library portfolio of two LGBTQ+ schools in the USA- Harvey Milk High School, in New York, and Pride School, formerly in Atlanta. Her memoirs continue to be reader favorites.

Joie has gone on to add a poetry book to her portfolio, Sapphoetry, and a beautiful coffee table book dedicated to the Orlando Pulse massacre victims, titled Cuarenta Y Nueve. Ms. Lamar was the visionary behind Cuarenta y Nueve, which means 49 in Spanish. The title was conceived because 49 innocent people lost their lives in this tragedy and because she organized 49 artists, of a multitude of disciplines, to contribute to the book. Joie contributed as part of the 49 artists as well.

While writing this novel, her first fiction, Ms. Lamar has also co-written a screenplay based on her memoir series. She is currently working towards further developing Las Alas, the screenplay, into a feature film and looking for production to begin in 2023/2024. As the great niece of the late Rafael Ramos - Cobian, famed Producer & Film

Maker, who built the first movie theatres and cinema chain in Puerto Rico and New York City, she is dedicated and honored to carry on in her family's tradition of bringing Latin film to the world.

www.brainspiredpublishing.com